The Fledgling

BY CARSON STASHWICK

bush
PUBLISHING
& associates

The Fledgling by Carson Stashwick

First publication in 2019 by Bush Publishing and Associates, LLC.

ISBN 978-1-944566-14-2

www.BushPublishing.com

Tulsa, Oklahoma

Cover Art by Jan McKay

Layout and Design by Bush Publishing and Associates, LLC.

Printed in the United States of America.

Disclaimer-Fiction

Other than actual historical events and public figures, all characters and incidents portrayed in this novel are fictitious. Any resemblance to actual persons, living or dead is purely coincidental.

For Eilie and Connor,

my favorite Fledglings

Acknowledgements

Writing a book is, mostly, a solitary endeavor. Getting a book into print, however, requires a multitude of talented people. Space limitations make it difficult to thank everyone who, at one time or another, had to endure incessant ramblings about my first novel. Yet, I would be remiss not to mention some outstanding individuals who took time to not only read draft after draft, but, also to provide critique and insight. In no particular order they include:

Mickey Allcock and Melody Palmer, librarians extraordinaire;

Beverly Simms Thompson, good friend and fellow writer;

Linda Clyburn, my irreplaceable sister-in-law, who sadly passed away;

Doug Hicks and JJ McKeever, professional writers, who offered a higher viewpoint;

Gina Lunsford and her 5th-Grade reviewers, who gave refreshing input;

Prism Budde and her mom, April, for their frank and amusing suggestions;

And, of course, Margo Bush, publisher, for allowing the Wingfield story to be told and truly giving Eilie her wings.

Contents

Prologue

The storm was as harsh as any the old priest could remember. He prayed aloud for the safety of his flock, and he prayed silently that he would live to see the morning. Almost the entire population of the village of Wingfield was huddled inside the church, kneeling, cowering at every thunderclap. This was no ordinary storm. It had raged for over two hours. To the villagers, there was an evil in the air they could not describe or explain. A sense of foreboding hung over them. To the simple people of Wingfield village in 1507, this was magic, and all magic was the work of the devil.

"Father, has God abandoned us?" called out a young girl in tears.

"God abandons no one!" the old priest assured her, trying very hard to assure himself.

The rain stopped abruptly, and the collective relief of a hundred frightened people could be felt. But now they were feeling something else, something unfamiliar; a vibration, like a drum getting louder until it seemed to be directly above them. The sky outside the church was getting lighter. It was not the quick flash of lightning, but a steady, growing light, as if the sun was rising eight hours too early. The sound and the light seemed to be joined and then suddenly, a sound louder than any heard in all of England shook them, and the light grew so bright the inside of the tiny stone church was as clear as day. Their fear of the storm was quickly replaced by the terror of the unknown. The earth moved, and every soul in the church believed it was the end of days.

It was not the end of days. Whatever it was, no one wanted to know. Their fear kept them clinging to each other, and no sound could be heard except some muffled sobs and the crying of an inconsolable baby. Everyone stayed close to the floor of the church fearful they were the only people left alive.

The congregation jumped in unison as the wooden door of the church flew open, and a large man hurried inside. Everyone recognized him; it was Joseph, the herdsman. "Father Matthew," he called out breathlessly, "I need you; I need you to come with me!"

Some of the men started to rise. "No, I only want Father Matthew. The rest of you stay here," Joseph said firmly. "Only the priest need see this. I do not know if this be from Heaven or Hell. You men, keep the women and children here for now. Father, please!" No one had ever heard Joseph say so many words. The force of what the normally quiet man said gave them a new fear. The old priest took a lantern from the altar and followed the herdsman outside. Two women rose and quickly closed the heavy door.

Joseph led the priest through the night over a grazing field less than a mile from the church. The ground was muddy and weighed their feet. The air smelled of fresh rain. But there was another scent; it was sharp and stung their noses. As they got close to a low wall, Father Matthew stopped in his tracks. "Joseph," he said, "In this darkness, I must have my directions turned. I do not remember this hillock."

"Aye, Father," Joseph responded. "You cannot remember what you've not seen. Until this hour that hillock was not here."

The priest moved the light closer. The hill was over twenty feet high and made of freshly turned soil. He noticed an opening into the hill and shuddered. *Has a door to Hell opened?* He thought to himself.

"Father," Joseph began slowly, "I saw it fall from the sky."

"What did you say, my son?" Father Matthew asked.

"I was under yon rocks," he said, pointing to a rocky outcrop on a nearby hill, "when the rain just stopped. I saw a light high in the sky. Not lightning, but like a lantern falling. This be no lantern, Father, for it were too big and hot. The light grew brighter, and I heard a noise that touched me bones. The light struck the ground here where we stand, and the ground shook fierce. I turned away for fear the devil had struck us. But then I says to meself, this not be the devil. The devil would come up from below, not from the sky. What say ye, Father. Does only God send fire from heaven? Is this a fallen star?"

The old priest pondered what Joseph had described. It could be a fallen star. He had seen many streak across the sky and marveled at the mysteries of creation. But to actually be standing where a star had fallen would be like getting a close look at God's handiwork. *Is this how all hillocks are formed?* he thought to himself. *Is every hillock the resting place of a fallen star?* He looked at Joseph and said, "I do not know with certainty if this is a fallen star, my son. But I do know with certainty that anything from Heaven is of God and we need not fear it."

The two men were not prepared for what happened next. A light came from inside the opening into the hill. They heard a hollow sound, like the clanging of a large pot. Looking toward the light, they could make out the figures of people coming from inside the hill. Joseph fell to his knees. Father Matthew could not speak. Nothing in his long life could explain what he saw. The figures drew closer. They were dressed in unfamiliar clothing that seemed to glow with the light behind them.

The old priest counted nine heads. Were they Angels? Were they Demons? His mind was racing, and he felt as if his heart would burst from his chest. Then the figure in front of the group held up a hand in a gesture of greeting. Father Matthew noticed the ones behind him seemed weak, unable to walk easily. Were they injured from their fall? Can Angels be harmed? He heard a voice, a clear, melodious voice saying, "Do not be afraid."

Father Matthew fell to his knees beside Joseph. He knew these words. He knew their meaning. He no longer doubted. These were Angels from God.

Chapter 1

Dreams

In our dreams we are able to fly... and that is a remembering of how we were meant to be.
- Madeleine L'Engle

The girl singing on the stage was very good. Her pitch was perfect, and the song she had chosen highlighted a voice much too mature for an eleven-year-old. Eilie Wingfield sat on the edge of her seat in the school auditorium and listened intently. Like many of the other elementary students watching the end-of-year talent show, Eilie was daydreaming that she was on stage wowing the audience with some special performance. It really wasn't fair, she thought, that some kids had the talent to sing or dance or both, and she couldn't even make a kazoo work. Still, she could imagine herself up on the stage taking a deep bow after a stunning performance. She just had no idea what that performance could be.

Eilie was the average height for a ten-year-old girl. Her weight was average. Her hair color was average. Even the length of her hair was average. For Eilie, that was the problem. Everything about her was average. She wanted to be more than average. She wanted to be as pretty as the girls on TV. She wanted to sing as well as the girls on the radio. She wanted to be good at something. Even in dance class, where she felt like a princess, she felt like an average princess.

She was pulled out of her daydream by a tap on her arm. It was her best friend, Francie Forbes. Eilie and Francie had been inseparable since kindergarten. Their teacher had seated them next to each other the first day. They were two scared little five-year-olds who took comfort from the sharing of this new adventure called 'school.' But more than just becoming fast friends, the two girls shared a unique bond. They soon discovered they each had old parents. Most of the kids at Riverview School in Tulsa, Oklahoma had parents who were in their twenties and thirties. Eilie's and Francie's parents were in their fifties. Their parents were the age of most of their classmates' grandparents.

"I think she's the last one," said Francie, pointing to the singer.

The girl finished her song, and the audience rewarded her with enthusiastic applause. As the curtain closed, Mrs. Clarkson, the school principal, walked to the microphone. "Weren't all our performers today just wonderful?" she said as she adjusted the microphone. "Let's give them all one more round of applause!" The curtain opened, and the talent show cast was lined up across the stage. They took a group bow as the curtain closed. "Before you all leave to enjoy your summer vacation, I want to thank each of our parents who were able to make it to our last talent show of this school year. And I want to remind you that our first show of the next school year will be the third Friday after the start of school. So, students, you have all summer to practice. And since all of our fifth graders are moving up to middle school next year, I expect we will see some exciting new talent at that show. Have a great summer, everyone. We'll see you back here in August."

The audience gave one more half-hearted round of applause and rose to start the slow move out of the auditorium. There were many hugs and good-byes being exchanged as the crowd filtered out the doors. Eilie and Francie held back, waiting for the crowd to clear a bit more before making their way to their parents standing by the exit.

"Just think," Eilie said, "next year we'll be fifth graders. We finally get to be the big kids."

"That will be so cool," Francie responded. "But then the next year we'll be the little kids again when we get to middle school."

"OK, so we have one year to rule," said Eilie.

Francie grabbed her friend's arm. "Did you tell your mom about your dreams yet?" she asked.

Eilie's face strained as she confessed she hadn't.

"You have got to tell your mom, Eilie," Francie said with deep concern.

"I know," said Eilie, "but she is so busy with her wedding plans that I just didn't want to bother her with it. Besides, they're just stupid dreams. They don't really mean anything."

Eilie's mom and dad had been divorced since she was three years old. Eilie spent half her time with her mom, the other half with her dad. It was an interesting arrangement, and for as long as she could remember, it was just the way things were. Each parent was a volunteer at Riverview School and, as much as possible, they were at every activity in which Eilie was involved. She really couldn't ask for a better mom or dad. They were just no longer married to each other.

When she was five years old, Eilie asked her mom why she and Daddy didn't live together. Her mom said that Daddy hadn't been honest with her; that he kept secrets. Her mom said that married people shouldn't keep secrets from each other. She explained that being married meant you had to be completely honest with each other. Eilie never believed her dad was dishonest. She remembered thinking that maybe Daddy was a spy and he just couldn't tell Mommy because he would be in danger. Sometimes, you think funny things when you're five.

"Well, if the dreams don't mean anything, then why have you been so freaked out about them?" asked Francie.

"Because they are so real," Eilie answered. "Everything is like I'm really there. I can feel the wind on my face and the wetness of a cloud. When I'm having the dreams, I'm really flying!"

"Are you sure Peter Pan isn't in those dreams?" Francie asked for the hundredth time.

"I told you before," Eilie said with a little impatience, "it's not a movie dream. It's just me flying through the air: just me and the sky. And sometimes, when I fly back to the ground, I stumble when I try to land, and the bump wakes me up. Taking off is easy, but landing is hard."

"Then if you don't tell your mom you should at least tell your dad," Francie protested.

"We're leaving next week for Uncle Jubal's ranch in Colorado," said Eilie. "I thought I would tell him about the dreams while we're driving."

"Will you get to ride horses and everything like last year?" Francie asked.

Eilie's face lit up at the memory. "You bet! Horseback riding is one of the best things at Tutela."

"What's Tutela?" Francie asked.

"That's what Uncle Jubal named his ranch," Eilie answered. "It's an old word that means protection or shelter or something. He likes old words that nobody uses anymore. He's got a dictionary that is so big it sits on its own table. I use the dictionary a lot when I visit Uncle Jubal."

"I guess old words are OK as long as they aren't on our vocabulary tests," Francie said. "How long will you get to stay at the ranch?"

"Two whole weeks," Eilie answered. "Daddy said we would have like a family reunion with a whole lot of Wingfields from all over the country. I'll even get to meet some cousins I haven't seen before. Maybe even some girls my age."

"I wish I could go and see the ranch," Francie said. "Then we could ride horses together."

"Sorry, but Uncle Jubal is really weird about only letting family come to Tutela," Eilie offered. She very much wanted to show Francie the ranch, but the rule was clear. "My mom said she and Daddy were married for five years before she ever got to go. Even then, she said she didn't feel like she was welcome there."

"Come on, girls. We've got to get going," Francie's mom called to them from the auditorium exit.

The girls looked up and waved at their parents. Frank and Katherine Forbes had been visiting with Eilie's parents near the back of the auditorium since the talent show ended. Jake and Carol Wingfield were outlining basic summer plans for getting the girls together; sleepovers, parties, swimming, all the important things parents of ten-year-old girls have to plan. The girls' families had been friends since those early kindergarten days when Eilie and Francie had decided they were sisters. Now, five years later, making arrangements for summer get-togethers was just a normal thing.

Frank and Katherine had never known the Wingfields as a couple, since Jake and Carol had been divorced before the girls ever met. Sometimes Carol would drop off Eilie at Francie's house; other times it would be Jake picking up Eilie. It was always just one of Eilie's parents at Francie's house, never both. So it was a rare occasion that all four of the parents were visiting at the same time.

"Carol, tell us more about your wedding," Katherine said. "When is it again?"

"August 5th," Carol answered. "You'll be getting an invitation soon. I hope you both can be there. And, of course, Eilie hopes Francie will be there so she won't be so bored."

"We'd love to come," Frank said. "So where did you meet... Paul, is it?"

"Paul Simmons," Carol said. "We met at a realtors' conference here in Tulsa. He's a mortgage banker."

"I'm sorry, Jake," Katherine interjected. "Is it uncomfortable for us to talk about this?"

"Not at all," Jake assured her. "I've met Paul, and I think he and Carol make a good match. Eilie seems to like him, so I don't have a problem with it. In fact, I'll be at the wedding."

Carol Wingfield owned a small real estate company and had spent the last several years building a reputation as a specialist in selling high-end houses. She dealt with clients who demanded results, and Carol delivered. She had five aggressive agents working for her who handled all the smaller homes the company contracted to sell.

Jake was an Associate Professor of History at the University of Tulsa and had published three books on American history. His students loved his classes on America from the 1880s to the 1920s. They were amazed at how his lectures seemed so personal and alive. Jake had a way of making history seem like it just happened yesterday.

The girls came running up to their parents with the usual string of requests; *Can I stay at her house? Can she stay at our house? Can we go get pizza?* Eilie's mom was the first to interrupt the dueling questions. "No, we need to stop by the grocery store on the way home," Carol said directly to Eilie. "Francie's parents and Dad and I have already discussed some times and places that you two can get together this summer. You'll have lots of time before school starts again."

"But, Mom," Eilie protested, "can't Francie spend the night before Daddy and me drive to Colorado?"

"You will spend this week with me and help with a few more details for the wedding," Carol began explaining. "Then next Thursday night you'll go to your dad's house, and you two will get to start your long drive Friday morning. You and Francie can have a sleepover when you get back from Colorado."

"That's three whole weeks!" Eilie said with the annoying whine she used when she thought a grown-up was being unfair.

"I think you and Francie can survive a three-week separation," Carol countered.

Francie moved close to Eilie and put a hand on her shoulder. "It's OK. Three weeks isn't that long," she said, trying to encourage her friend. "Besides, we'll have lots of stories to tell in three weeks."

The girls hugged, the men shook hands, and everyone said goodbye as they headed toward their cars. Jake walked Eilie and Carol to the parking lot. "Alright, I will come get you on Thursday, and we will get everything packed for the trip. Give me a hug, Little," Jake said to Eilie.

"I'm not little anymore," Eilie complained as she and her dad hugged. She felt that his nickname for her was no longer fitting.

"You'll always be little to me," Jake replied. "I love you."

"I love you, too, Daddy," Eilie conceded.

Across from the school parking lot, a man in a black SUV was watching through binoculars as Eilie's dad got into one car, and Eilie and her mom got into another. The man was wearing a dark suit and dark glasses. He picked up a cell phone and keyed in a number. A gruff voice answered, "Yes."

"They're leaving the school now," said the man in the dark suit.

"Good," the gruff voice said. "Everything he's doing is so predictable. Let me know if anything unusual happens before they leave next Friday. Otherwise, just have your men keep him under surveillance. We'll grab them in Colorado, before they get to the ranch."

Chapter 2

Secrets

Real flight and dreams of flight go together. Both
are part of the same movement.
                                    -Thomas Pynchon

The wind was flowing briskly around her face as she
willed herself to move toward a distant cloud. Her feet
dangled loosely, and she was keenly aware of the ground a
hundred feet below. Nothing held her up except the sheer
joy of flying. Eilie Wingfield was flying. She knew how to fly
as naturally as she knew how to breathe. She felt her long,
brown hair flowing behind her, and she sensed that she was
moving forward at a speed equivalent to riding a bicycle.

Looking below, she could see the fields neatly laid out in
a patchwork quilt pattern. She recognized the terrain. She
was following the Arkansas River westward out of Tulsa.
She remembered the scenery from when she and her dad
had taken a helicopter ride over the Keystone Dam just five
miles further. She would never consider walking five miles,
but flying was easier than walking. Eilie knew she could

make it to Lake Keystone and not even break a sweat. She was unafraid, and a welcome feeling of peace was wrapping itself around her.

Without warning, she felt a sharp pain on both sides of her lower back. It was a burning pain, like the kind she would get in her stomach if she ran too fast for too long. She stopped in mid-air. The pain seemed to be growing, and she was having trouble catching her breath. Then, she felt a strong pull downward. Gravity was taking hold. She began to fall. She looked down and saw the ground rushing up toward her. She was no longer upright, but tumbling through the air, and nothing was going to catch her. The ground below looked hard and unforgiving. She suddenly felt afraid and screamed.

The sound of her own scream woke her. Eilie realized she had been dreaming. She had not hit the ground, but she was lying on the floor of her room across from her bed, and she had no idea how she got there. Underneath her was a pile of scattered books, and one of her bookcases was knocked over on the floor. The pain in her back was gone, but she felt a new pain in her left wrist.

The door to the bedroom flew open, and Eilie saw her mom staring in shocked disbelief. The sudden realization of pain and fear gripped Eilie, and she welled up with tears. "Mommy," she called out. "I think my arm is broken."

Carol rushed to her, stepping over books and stuffed animals which, just minutes earlier, had been in their proper places on the now topsy-turvy bookcase. "Honey, what happened? Were you climbing the bookshelves?"

"I don't know," Eilie said, wiping away tears with her right hand, trying very hard not to move her left.

"Let me see your arm," Carol commanded, feigning calm while her heart was pounding and her thoughts were racing. She glanced across the room, trying to imagine how Eilie pulled over a six-foot-tall bookcase and injured herself. It made no sense to Carol; Eilie was not prone to sleepwalking.

Eilie squeaked out, "It hurts really bad," before breaking into full-blown sobbing.

Carol managed to gather her thoughts long enough to allow reason to overcome panic. Looking directly at Eilie, she said, "Here's what we are going to do. I will change out of my pajamas, and we will get into the car and drive to the emergency room. I'll call your dad on the way. You stay here while I gather my things. I'll be right back. Okay?"

"Okay," Eilie whimpered.

In a dark basement, a machine began glowing. The light it emitted bounced off the walls of the room. Had anyone been in the room to see, the outline of the small, exploratory craft would have been plainly visible. But no one was in the room. And, had anyone been in the room to hear, they would have heard a distinct, low voice say, "A mutation is detected. I need verification of purpose. Please respond." The machine waited but received no response. "I need verification of purpose. Please respond." Several minutes passed and still no response. Then the voice said, "Open the Quortrin."

Five-hundred-seventy miles above the Earth, a silent sentinel suddenly awoke. The large craft was circling the globe in a polar orbit. It heard the call and responded, "Quortrin stands ready. I await your instructions."

"Sartrin reports the detection of a mutation. Please scan for other crew members and report."

The large, black craft adjusted its angle and emitted a wide beam across the surface of the planet below. "Full scan will require two passes. I will report results when completed."

On the planet surface, an alert bell rang on the console of Tech Sergeant Carlos Sanchez's workstation at the NORAD complex. It was an unfamiliar alarm. Sergeant Sanchez grabbed his codebook and quickly flipped through the laminated pages trying to determine what the bell was telling him. He turned down the volume and turned to his commanding officer. "Major Westin, Sir. I cannot identify the source of this alarm. I can't find it anywhere in my guide."

Major Westin looked up from his computer screen. "Repeat that, Sergeant," he said.

"Sir, I do not know what this alarm is for," the young, non-commissioned officer confessed. "I cannot respond appropriately because I do not know the alarm."

Major Westin rose from his desk and went to the sergeant's workstation. He looked at the old-style flashing light positioned on the oldest console on the satellite monitoring floor. An unexpected realization froze him.

"What is it, sir?" Sanchez asked. "How should I respond?"

"This one is above my pay grade, Sergeant," the major answered. He turned toward the Command Platform positioned a half-floor above the Monitoring Center and called out, "Colonel, sir. We need you over here, please. It appears the Black Knight is active."

From across the large room, where NORAD monitors all 15,000 man-made objects circling the planet, a dry and unimpressed voice responded, "I don't have time for jokes, Major."

"I assure you, sir, I am not joking," Major Westin said. "The Black Knight is transmitting."

Sergeant Sanchez looked up at Major Westin and asked, "Sir, what is the Black Knight?"

"We're not really sure," he answered. "It's apparently been in orbit around the Earth since before we ever launched satellites into space. According to legend, it was first detected when Nicola Tesla intercepted a radio signal from it in the 1890s. We have pictures of it taken from shuttle missions. We know it's not ours and we're pretty sure it's not Russian or Chinese. We've been monitoring it for over 50 years. But this is the first time it has shown any activity."

"I don't understand, sir. Are you saying there is an alien satellite in orbit?" Sergeant Sanchez asked.

"I'm not going to speculate on that, Sergeant," the major answered. "But for something to maintain a polar orbit for this long, with no sign of decay, is unusual."

The colonel descended the steps of his elevated platform and approached the workstation. He stood silent for a moment, staring at the flashing red light and then said, "Sergeant, turn off the alarm. I'll analyze the data from my computer and determine if we have anything to be concerned about. Carry on, gentlemen." The colonel returned to the upper platform and began a signal analysis program.

"Major, Sir, if this satellite has never transmitted before, why do we have a wave sensor focused on it with an alarm?" the sergeant asked.

"Because somewhere back in the 1960s some paranoid senator learned about its being there and insisted that it should be monitored in case it was a cleverly disguised Russian spy satellite," Major Westin answered. "So for more than 50 years, we have tracked it. The military first stumbled onto it while we were tracking Sputnik in the late fifties. At first, they thought it was a natural satellite, like an asteroid. When scientists realized it was not natural, they had to explain how it got there and where it came from. That's when all the crazy theories started."

"How big is it?" Sergeant Sanchez asked.

"That's the strangest thing of all. It's huge. No nation on Earth had the technology to put something that big into space back then," the major explained. "We don't know where it came from or how it got there. All we know is, it's there, and it just circles the globe like a dutiful soldier. That's why it's called the Black Knight, like it's watching over us. If you want to get really scared just read some of the things written about it on the web."

"As soon as I'm off duty, I will," Sanchez said.

The colonel returned to the workstation and held up a chart showing several signal readings intersecting a portion of the sky. "It seems we have a false alarm, gentlemen," he began explaining. "What I see here is an echo signal bouncing off the Black Knight, apparently from this communications satellite, as it passed close by. Our mysterious Black Knight will remain a mystery. There is nothing here to indicate it is transmitting. Any questions?"

Major Westin and Tech Sergeant Sanchez looked closely at the chart and nodded in agreement. "Thank you, sir. I think that clears it up," Major Westin said as he returned to his computer near the center of the room.

"Colonel, sir, have we really been watching this thing for over fifty years?" Sanchez asked. "Could it be alien?"

"I think it's just a remnant of a rocket or some other space debris that's been misidentified," the colonel said. "You know how many man-made objects we monitor from here, son. Do you really think there could be an alien craft in orbit around our planet and we wouldn't know about it?"

"I guess you're right, Sir," the sergeant conceded. "It would be impossible to hide something like that from our sensors. I'm sorry we troubled you, Sir."

"Not a problem, Sergeant," the colonel assured him. "But next time, just turn off the alarm. We don't need to waste our time chasing ghosts."

"Yes, Sir," Tech Sergeant Sanchez said. "Thank you, Colonel."

It was just before midnight when Carol led Eilie through the door of the ER at Saint Francis Hospital. After a remarkably short wait, Eilie and her mom were taken into an examination area with privacy curtains; as if any emergency room has privacy.

Eilie was no stranger to the ER. She had been brought here one memorable Halloween night when she was six years old. While out Trick-or-Treating with her dad, she suddenly was bent over with a horrible pain in her side. Before the next morning, the doctors had removed her ruptured appendix.

But the peculiar thing was what the surgeon told her parents after the operation. He said that the rupture had been encapsulated. Eilie didn't understand what he meant, but her dad later explained that somehow her body had built a wall around her appendix, so the infection from the rupture would not poison her. He said that her appendix had actually ruptured about five days earlier. The doctor said he could not explain why she had not died from appendicitis.

A nurse came in. "You must be Ellie," he started.

"It's 'Eye Lee,'" Carol and Eilie said together. It was a lifelong chore for the Wingfields to correct other people's mispronunciation of Eilie's simple Irish name. It was always new teachers or adults who read her name but never really saw the first i after the first c.

"E-i-l-i-e," Eilie spelled out for him. She was proud of her name and annoyed at adults who couldn't read.

"I am sorry," the young nurse offered. "My name is Geoff, G-e-o-f-f," he said, pointing to the name tag on his scrubs. "Everybody who hears my name wants to spell it J-e-f-f and everybody who reads it wants to pronounce it Jee Off. So I completely understand your frustration."

Eilie liked this guy. He made her feel more relaxed, and he was not overbearing. He winked at her, and the coldness of the room seemed to warm. "So, Miss Eilie," he said, drawing out her name in correct pronunciation, "what happened to your arm?"

"I guess I fell out of bed and landed on it," she said half as a statement and half as a question.

"You don't sound too convinced," the nurse replied.

"I was asleep, so I don't know for sure," Eilie countered.

"Well, before the doctor gets here, I need to weigh you and take your blood pressure. Is that OK?" he asked.

Eilie nodded yes. The pain wasn't quite so strong now in her wrist, but she was beginning to feel the pain in her lower back again. The nurse helped Eilie toward the scale. Holding her injured arm close to her belly, she stepped onto the scale and felt a tingling all over like she got when her arm fell asleep.

"Well, that's weird," Geoff said, tapping on the scale. "According to this you only weigh thirteen pounds. I'll go get an old fashioned scale. This digital screen must be broken."

By the time Jake got to the ER, Eilie and her mom were in the waiting room. Eilie's wrist was wrapped, and her arm was in a sling. Jake went straight to his daughter and hugged her. "Hey, Little. Mom said you might have broken your arm. What happened?"

Eilie tried very hard not to cry in front of her dad. It was easy to cry with Mom, but Daddy was different. Of course, she had cried many times with her dad, but as she was getting older, she found herself thinking of him as more of an authority figure than a confidant. With Mom, she could share girl talk and secrets. She could tell her mom about boys she liked. She just didn't feel comfortable sharing those things with her dad. Despite her best efforts, Eilie buried her face into her dad's chest and started crying.

Carol took the cue to answer Jake's question. "There was no break, but her wrist is badly sprained. We have a prescription for some pain medicine, and the ER doctor said we should take her to see the pediatrician on Monday about her kidneys."

"What's wrong with her kidneys?" Jake asked.

"Eilie complained that they have been hurting off-and-on all night," Carol responded. "The doctor thought she should be checked out for a kidney infection, so I'll make an appointment with Dr. Elephant." (Eilie's pediatrician was not named Dr. Elephant. His real name was Oliphant, and he had been her doctor since she was born. But as Eilie learned to talk, she was not quite able to say his name correctly, so it became Dr. Elephant.)

Jake pulled a handkerchief from his pocket and wiped his daughter's eyes. "So, how did you fall?" he asked.

"I don't know," Eilie answered.

"The strange thing is that she somehow knocked over a bookcase. I don't know if she was sleepwalking, but she could not have fallen out of bed and ended up across the room on top of a bookcase," Carol explained.

Jake was frowning as he processed the information he was hearing. "Eilie, show me exactly where you felt the pain in your kidneys."

Eilie turned around and pointed to the spots on either side of her lower back where the pain had plagued her. Jake turned her back around and put his hand on his daughter's shoulder. Looking deeply into her eyes, he asked, "Have you been dreaming about flying?"

Eilie's mouth dropped open. She slowly nodded yes. She saw an expression on her dad's face she had never seen before. It was almost as if she could hear his thoughts. As her dad turned back toward her mom, his expression changed, and Eilie got the strange feeling that he was about to tell a lie.

"Well, I think I have figured out this little mystery," he said to Carol.

"What do you mean?" she asked.

"Eilie was dreaming that she was flying. She got out of bed and climbed up the book shelves while still asleep. As she got higher up, she shifted the balance of the bookcase, and it came crashing down with her. Her arm got between the falling bookcase and the floor and was sprained." Jake turned back toward Eilie. "A very similar thing happened to me when I was your age. But I got a knot on my head. It took two weeks for it to go down."

Carol thought through what Jake had said. "I guess that's as good an explanation as any," she said. "But why flying? Couldn't she have been dreaming about mountain climbing?"

"I remember dreaming about flying as a kid," Jake answered. "I would wake up in a different room."

"So you sleep walked as a child?" Carol asked.

Jake smiled. "More than once, but I soon outgrew it. I don't think we'll have to worry about Eilie doing it again, though. Listen, Carol, I know you have a lot on your plate right now. I will be happy to take Eilie to see Dr. Oliphant on Monday to have her kidneys checked out before our trip. And since her arm is going to be in a sling for the next few days, she won't be as much help as you had hoped. I'll pick her up tomorrow and look after her so you can focus on the wedding."

"I don't know," Carol pondered. "Eilie, Honey, what do you think? Do you want to get dragged all over town with me, or do you want to spend some more time with your dad?"

Looking at her dad, Eilie saw that strange new expression again. "I'll go with Daddy," she said.

"Great," Jake said. "It is almost two AM. Why don't you two go home and get some sleep. It's been a busy night for both of you. I'll pick you up before noon, and we'll go out for a burger or something." He bent down to kiss his daughter on the cheek and whispered in her ear, "You will sleep well tonight, Little. No more dreams. I promise."

Eilie wasn't sure why, but she believed her dad was right. *But how did he know?*

Chapter 3

Mysteries

Man must rise above the Earth - to the top of the atmosphere and beyond - for only thus will he fully understand the world in which he lives.

- Socrates

Jake Wingfield found it hard to sleep. He had crawled into bed at three AM, and now, four hours later, he was still awake. He tried to organize his thoughts. There was much to do, and he wasn't quite sure where to start. It had been years since anything had kept him awake all night. In fact, his last all-nighter was the day his beautiful baby girl was born.

Eilie came into the world and into Jake's life one bright, cold, Saturday morning in December, ten years ago. He had felt helpless and useless in trying to comfort his wife through a grueling thirty-six-hour labor; having her first child at the age of forty-five was difficult for Carol. All his life, Jake had dreamed of having a daughter, and the reality of Eilie's birth hit him like a ton of bricks. *Was he prepared for this? Could he be a good dad? Could he protect her? Would she be normal?*

That last question haunted him most. And now, ten years later, he was processing the consequences of the answer. The events that unfolded just hours ago brought into sharp focus the responsibility he now faced. He knew everything had changed, and he knew he had to deal with it. He just wasn't sure he could.

How do you explain to a ten-year-old that she is different? Not just different from her friends, but different from everyone. How do you prepare a little girl to assume an adult responsibility? How do you begin to groom her to be unique in her world? And, most importantly, how do you tell that little girl's mother the secret that led to your divorce?

Jake and Carol had met over twenty years ago when they were both attending graduate school at the University of Oklahoma. Carol was working on her MBA, and Jake was finishing his Masters in history. Carol used to joke that Jake talked about history like he had lived it. He had been teaching at the community college in Tulsa and had planned to go east after he got his advanced degree to teach at the university level in some small New England school. Carol convinced him to apply to teach at the University of Tulsa. He did and was hired to teach freshman classes.

After a couple of years of off-and-on dating, they married and set up house in Tulsa. Seven years later, Eilie was born. By then, Jake had earned his doctorate degree in history, and Carol had an established real estate business. Everything was as good as Jake could hope for. But sometimes things are not as good as they seem and friction developed between them; mostly around Jake's unusual relationship with his extended family.

To Carol, Jake seemed too devoted to the affairs of his relatives and not focused enough on his wife and daughter. He would spend hours on the phone with family members she had never met. He volunteered to write family histories and contributed material to the family genealogy website. But the breaking point for Carol was Jake's refusal to explain it all; she felt left out. She resented that conversations would change when she entered the room. She became aware of hushed tones and whispered exchanges to which she was not included. By the time Eilie was three, the marriage was over.

The one thing each of them remained devoted to was their daughter. They were old enough to understand that Eilie, like any child, deserved both parents. So, they pledged not to let their divorce do any more harm to Eilie than necessary. No child escapes their parents' divorce unscathed, but Eilie had it easier than most; she was very young when it happened, and she was never truly separated from either parent.

Jake remembered bringing Eilie home from the hospital, holding her through the first night. For several weeks after, even though she was one of the rare babies who slept through the night, Jake would wake every hour and check to make sure she was alright. He began to doubt his sanity for becoming a father at his age. Eventually, he became more relaxed and got more sleep.

Jake let out a large sigh as he thought about the last ten years and the benchmarks of Eilie's life; her first tooth, first steps, first bicycle, first pony ride, first day of school, first kitten. And now, she was about to experience the biggest 'first' of all. He picked up his cell phone and carefully composed the text he had hoped he would never have to send; *A Fledgling has perched.*

He understood what he needed to do but was suddenly awash with a sense of defensiveness. He had a biological imperative to protect his daughter. And he would, even if it meant protecting her from her own family.

The cell phone beeped. Jake read the incoming text. *She is only 10. This would make her the youngest ever. Any witnesses?*

Jake keyed in his answer. *No, but injured wrist in fall. She'll be OK for Gathering.*

His cell phone screen read; *Good news. The Clan will be pleased. It's been over 140 years since the last.*

"Yeah, I remember," Jake said out loud. "I was there."

Jubal Wingfield laid down his cell phone and pondered the text he'd just read. He had worked out every detail of the

Gathering, but now he had to factor in an unplanned twist. He had to determine the best way to present a Fledgling to the Clan. Over one hundred family members would be converging on his ranch in less than a week, and he wanted the Gathering to be perfect. Presenting a Fledgling would be the icing on the cake.

Jubal stood up from his desk. His six-foot frame was lean, and he looked to be a man in his sixties. There was a touch of gray in his light brown hair, and the crow's feet around his eyes betrayed his normally unworried look. Beneath his white cotton shirt, the faint outline of well-developed muscles could be seen. He held himself with confidence, and his bearing was that of a military man reflecting decades of personal discipline. It was this discipline that had kept him alive all these years.

It was six-fifteen AM in Colorado, an earlier time zone than Tulsa, and the air just north of Telluride was crisp and cool. Early June at this elevation was still cold compared to the rest of the country.

Jubal grabbed a legal pad and started making notes. He had to be sure not to overlook any detail. After putting his major thoughts on paper, he tapped the keyboard of his desktop computer. The oversized screen came to life, and a pleasant female voice said, "Good morning, Jubal. How may I help you?"

"Good morning, Gracie," he responded.

GRACIE was a computer software program Jubal created; **General Response and Cognitive Intelligence Exploration.** The program was designed to go beyond normal voice recognition technology. It was a search engine with syntax-based protocols combined with true artificial intelligence. It could learn the language patterns of whoever was speaking to it and understand meaning beyond words. Normal word-based search engines only give responses to the specific word typed or spoken. You might ask for information about 'cough syrup' and get millions of responses using the word 'cough' and the word 'syrup.' The responses would include 'pancake syrup' and 'cough drops,' neither of which was specifically, 'cough syrup.'

GRACIE was able to scour the entire world-wide-web and pull all references to 'cough syrup.' She would then ask, "What kind of cough are you experiencing?" and continue to ask questions until she accurately diagnosed your cough. Then she would scrub the websites of every cough syrup manufacturer by replacing the website's HTML coding with her own so she 'knew' everything on the site. With pinpoint accuracy, she would find the specific cough syrup needed for your specific cough, and then search the websites of distributors or retailers and find where the medicine could be ordered. She would select the best site, order the medicine with your credit card, and the cough syrup would be delivered to your door the next day. Most amazing of all, GRACIE did all this in less than five seconds; in sixty different languages if needed.

"Gracie, I need a family member file," Jubal began.

"I have already pulled up Eilie Wingfield's file," Gracie interjected. "I was monitoring your text communication with Jake."

"Of course you were," he retorted.

"The file is onscreen or, if you prefer, I can read it to you," Gracie offered.

"I'll read it onscreen, thank you," Jubal said.

He sat back down at his desk and began reading Eilie's file, which included everything from birth to her visit to the ER just six hours ago. It wasn't a large file, but it was thorough. Every detail of her life from school grades to Girl Scouts was recorded. Simply put, any reference to Eilie Wingfield on any computer on Earth was found by GRACIE and compiled into a personal dossier. GRACIE could do this on any subject or any individual. She did this leaving no trace of her prying, and she did it with incredible speed. No one could hide from GRACIE, and no one knew she existed.

Jubal finished reading and closed his eyes. He thought about the perfection of timing. For Eilie to perch just before the Gathering was lucky. But 'luck' was not a concept Jubal believed in. To him, the coincidence almost seemed like destiny. It had been ten years since the last Gathering. Jake was not able to attend then because he and his wife had an infant to look after. And now that child would be formally introduced to the Clan as a Fledgling. Eilie had visited the ranch the last two summers, but she had never been to a Gathering. She had not yet met the Clan. And all she knew about Jubal was that he was her dad's uncle. She had no idea who he really was.

"Jubal," Gracie intoned.

He opened his eyes and answered, "Yes."

If it is possible for a computer voice to sound worried, Gracie did when she said, "We have a problem."

"What kind of problem?" Jubal asked.

Gracie was not prone to emotion or hyperbole. She was the most efficient computer program on the planet, and she had access to information countries would kill for. For her to express a problem meant that she had run into a situation or found information she could not analyze. Although she was incapable of pride, she found herself perplexed at the possibility that she could not unravel a twisted bit of data. "While assembling the file on Eilie, I ran an algorithm designed to seek out all references to her combined names and then filtered out all non-pertinent information...,"

"Yes, Gracie," Jubal interrupted. "I am very aware of the methods you use. What did you find?"

"I found that someone else has been looking for Eilie and Jake using almost identical methods," Gracie answered. "Whoever has been searching has primarily sought information on Jake. They have even scrubbed his appointment calendar on his office computer. There is a data residue -- I can best describe as fingerprints -- found in the places where the search was conducted. I don't believe the searcher knows he left fingerprints, and I am currently running a program that should lead us back to the spy."

"Well, old girl," Jubal said with a hint of an English accent, "you've been busy. And so has someone else, but who?"

"I will alert you as soon as I know the answer," Gracie assured him.

"I know you will, Gracie," he added with confidence. "Do a quick check on the Wingfield Family Society website and see if there are any traces of our spy there, please."

The Wingfield Family Society is a highly organized group of people across the world who not only share the same surname but also have a keen interest in their family history. The Wingfield family traces its roots back to medieval England and Wingfield Castle. The castle is still standing, although parts of it have been removed over time. Among its more notable family members, the Society lists Major WC Wingfield, the inventor of tennis, and Captain Edward-Maria Wingfield, first President of Jamestown Colony and one of the founders of Virginia. The Society hosts annual reunions across America and abroad. However, Jubal's Gatherings tended to be very select, and much more private.

"Bingo!" Gracie announced. "Whoever we are dealing with has been all over the site. I even see some snooping in the Administrator's pages. But, the most obvious searching has been on your particular branch of the family tree. And, Jubal, the texts between you and Jake this morning were read as well. "

"Well, it looks as if we have a bit of a mystery," Jubal said. "Gracie, how can I get a message to Jake without our spy reading or hearing it?"

"The only solution to delivering a message that does not involve electronic devices is a private courier," Gracie replied.

"Thank you for making everything so simple, Gracie," said Jubal. He grabbed his cell phone, hit a pre-set number and spoke into the phone, "Can you meet me at the stables in fifteen minutes? Good. I'll explain then." He ended the call and got up from his desk. Jubal did not tend to pace or show any other outward signs of stress, so it caught him by surprise when he realized he was whistling out loud. Fortunately, there was no one there to hear him but Gracie, and she was occupied with her search for the mystery spy. Despite his worry, Jubal was aware of a tinge of excitement, and he thought to himself that things were about to get interesting.

His cell phone rang, interrupting his train of thought. "Hello," he answered.

"Jubal, this is Charlie," the caller said.

"Well, it seems to be the day for surprises," Jubal responded. "How are you, Charlie?"

"I'm fine, thanks," Charlie answered. "We picked up a transmission a few hours ago. Are you aware of any activity from above?"

"You're certain of the source?" Jubal asked.

"Yes, I verified it myself," the caller replied.

"Thanks for letting me know," Jubal said. "I'll look into it and keep you informed."

"I would appreciate that," he said.

"Of course," Jubal responded. "And Charlie, be careful. Please."

"This ain't my first rodeo, Jubal," he replied.

Chapter 4

Answers

> *Be like the bird in flight... pausing a while on boughs too slight, feels them give away beneath her, yet sings, knowing yet that she has wings.*
> *- Victor Hugo*

Jake rang the doorbell at Carol's house. Eilie answered the door and ran into her father's arms, being careful not to bump her injured wrist.

"Daddy, you were right!" she said with a big smile. "I didn't have any more dreams about flying." Then, almost in a whisper, she asked, "How did you know I wouldn't?"

"We'll talk about it later, Little," he quietly answered. "We have a lot to talk about."

Carol Wingfield came to the door rolling a large suitcase. "I know you will probably pack another bag of things she has at your house, but I gathered up clothes and items I thought she might need for a two-week trip to the ranch," she said. "Are you still planning on leaving next Friday morning?"

"Yes," Jake answered. "I have a few more work items to clear off my desk before we go."

Carol handed Jake a pill bottle. "Here's the pain medicine for her wrist. She gets one pill every twelve hours. And she needs to leave the sling on for at least a week."

"It doesn't hurt as much," Eilie interjected.

"Good to hear," Jake said to Eilie. "I'll try to get her in to see Dr. Oliphant as soon as possible to make sure she doesn't have a kidney infection. But it occurred to me that the pain she was feeling may have just been from the fall." He looked at Eilie and asked, "Have you had any more pain in your back, Honey?"

Carol cut in, "The medicine would ease kidney pain along with the wrist pain. So, she still needs to be checked out for an infection."

Well, I tried, Jake thought to himself. "Good point. I'll call the doctor's office Monday morning." He knew the cause of Eilie's back pain was not a kidney infection. He also knew he needed to go through the motions of pretending not to know. If that meant an unnecessary trip to the doctor, then so be it.

"Will you please call me and let me know what the doctor says?" Carol asked. Looking at Eilie, she added, "And will you please remind your dad to call me after the doctor visit?"

"Yes, Ma'am," Eilie said with a sharp salute.

Carol laughed. "Oh, stop it. Give me a hug."

Eilie and her mom hugged goodbye as the hall clock was chiming noon. Jake headed toward the car with the suitcase. Eilie quickly followed and got into the front passenger seat. Jake watched her struggle a bit with the seatbelt and asked, "Do you need help with that?"

"No," she answered. "Besides, I've got to do a lot of things with one arm for a while, so I need the practice." She buckled her seatbelt and gave a big sigh. "OK," she said. "I have some questions."

Jake put the car in reverse and pulled out of the driveway. He looked at Eilie with a grin that reflected both amusement and pride. Ever since she was old enough to talk, Eilie had demonstrated a strong will. She was never bashful about expressing herself, at least not to her parents. Jake knew he had no choice but to answer all her questions. But, he wanted to provide the answers at a measured pace so she could slowly grasp the finer points of what he had to tell her. The last thing he wanted was to give her too much information too fast. "OK," he said, "Ask away."

"First question," Eilie started, "Am I an alien?"

Jake's mouth suddenly got very dry, but he managed to answer, "Yes."

Eilie's eyes were wide, and she stared at her dad in disbelief. "That was not the answer I expected," she said.

"And that was not the question I expected," Jake shot back. "How did you jump to that conclusion?"

"I was just thinking that none of my friends dream about flying, and you knew I was even though I never told you, and you lied to Mom when you told her you knew how I hurt my arm, and this morning I floated in the shower, oh my gosh," Eilie took a breath, "I'm an alien!"

"OK, Honey. Slow down. Really? You floated in the shower?" he asked. "Did you tell your mom about that?"

Eilie shook her head 'no' while biting her lip.

"Good. We probably shouldn't say anything to her just yet. Let's take this one step at a time," Jake said, trying to gather his thoughts. "First, you're not a hundred percent alien. Neither am I. We are descended from a group of travelers who were stranded on Earth a long time ago. Our original family came from a planet billions of miles away. They crashed in England and over time adopted the name of the place where they were stranded. They eventually accepted that they could not return to their homeworld and blended into the human community. The aliens married humans, and children were born who were half-human and half-alien. Are you following me so far?"

Eilie nodded yes. "Is Mom an alien?"

Jake let out a chuckle and answered, "No, just you and me." He took a breath and continued, "Honey, there are certain things about our family, my side of the family, that you're going to learn in the next few days and I don't want any of this to scare you. The Clan, our family, has been on Earth over 500 years. We arrived before humans had electricity, or cars, or even indoor plumbing. We have certain traits, certain abilities that humans don't."

"We can fly," Eilie added.

"We can fly," her father repeated, "But, not all of us. There are some descendants who did not inherit the ability. Have you learned about genes in school?"

"The kind you wear or the kind that decide if you get blue eyes or brown eyes?" Eilie asked.

Jake laughed. "The kind you wear is spelled j-e-a-n-s. The kind that determines eye color is spelled g-e-n-e-s."

"We learned that two blue-eyed people can have blue-eyed babies, but if the mom or dad has brown eyes, the baby probably won't have blue eyes," she proudly remembered.

"That's a great example," Jake encouraged. "Genes are bits of information we carry inside every cell of our bodies. They determine the color of eyes, hair, and skin. They give our bodies the information to be tall or short, skinny or big, and whether we have straight hair or curly hair. Or, as in the case of your mom's cousin, Steve, they determine whether or not we get to keep our hair. When our alien side of the family combined genes with the human side of the family, the offspring got a mix of different traits. So, not every Wingfield can fly."

"But it looks like I got the flying genes," Eilie said with a bit of pride and uncertainty.

Jake gave a small grin and asked, "Does that scare you?"

"A little, I guess," she answered. "Why did I dream about flying before I really flew?"

"That's because of your alien genes," Jake began. "Every person on the homeworld is able to fly, but usually not until they are about 20 years old. Imagine what a problem it would be for babies to fly out of their cribs, or toddlers to fly off chasing a balloon. It would be dangerous for children to be able to fly, like a bird that hasn't yet grown all its feathers jumping out of the nest. So as a survival mechanism, our people weren't able to fly until they reached a certain level of maturity. What would happen if you let a five-year-old drive a car?"

"They would crash and be hurt or killed," Eilie was quick to reason.

"Exactly. So, in preparation to fly, our people started dreaming about flying a few weeks before their flight organs matured, usually before their twentieth birthday. This gave them the opportunity to practice without risk. Like playing a video game about driving a car," he added.

Eilie was eagerly taking in all the information her dad was giving. She wanted to understand everything, yet she was still unsure that any of it was real. She tried to imagine what actual flying would be like. If it was like the dreams, then she was ready to fly now. She wanted to tell her dad to stop the car and let her fly the rest of the way to his house. She thought about what he had just explained and asked, "What are flight organs?"

"Remember the pain you've been feeling around your kidneys?" Jake asked. "First, an organ is a specialized group of cells that have a specific job to perform. Your kidneys filter waste from your blood. Your heart pumps blood throughout your body to get oxygen to every cell. Your eyes give you the ability to see. These are organs. A flight organ is what enables our people to overcome the pull of gravity and fly. You have two, one above each of your two kidneys. They are connected to your adrenal glands. The adrenal glands produce a hormone called adrenaline. When we get scared, adrenaline is released into the blood, and it causes our hearts to beat faster."

"You mean the 'flight or fight' reaction?" asked Eilie.

"Yes, but on our planet, it literally was 'flight,'" Jake answered. "Our ancient ancestors on the homeworld developed an extra gland that worked in conjunction with the adrenal gland. This gland, the ascendal gland, creates an abatement field around our cells, which overcomes gravity and allows us to fly away from danger. Abatement means to counteract, to do away with."

"Why does it hurt?" she asked with a look of worry that flying would not be as fun as she had hoped.

"It only hurts the first four or five times. As the glands reach maturity, they begin excreting ascendaline, and the process is new and painful. That's why you complained about your back hurting, and the ER doctor thought you might have a kidney infection. What probably happened last night, before you hurt your arm, was you were dreaming about flying. During the dream, your ascendal glands activated and you floated around your room. You felt the pain, and it caused you to flinch; you lost your ascendaline and fell, knocking over the bookcase on the way to the floor. When I was twelve, I landed headfirst on the arm of a chair and got a knot the size of an egg on my forehead."

"Wait a minute," Eilie interrupted. "You said we don't start flying until we're about twenty because it would be dangerous for kids to fly. But you were twelve, and I'm ten. Why are you and me different?"

"It goes back to genes again, Little," Jake explained. "On our homeworld, nobody started flying until they were out of their teens. But, occasionally, a child would develop their flying abilities a little earlier than most. The youngest I know of from our home was fifteen. But when the travelers were stranded here and mixed their genes with humans, some unexpected results occurred. There were some mutations, changes within the genes, which resulted in some unplanned consequences. Some of the children developed mature ascendal glands at a younger age; as early as twelve. But so far, no one has started as early as you. You are the youngest of us to fledge."

Eilie got her usual expression upon hearing a new word. "What does fledge mean?" she asked.

"It's when a young bird leaves the nest. A fledgling is a bird almost ready to fly, but it still needs help from its parents. It will perch on the edge of the nest and flap its wings. It waits for instinct to kick in so it can overcome its fear and do what it was born to do; fly. A fledgling is a young bird on the edge of flight."

"You were a Fledgling, Daddy?" she asked.

"Yes," Jake answered. "And for the longest time, I was the youngest. But now you are."

"Will you teach me how to make it work? I want to fly," Eilie said with a pleading expression.

"You'll have lots of time to learn. And when we get to Uncle Jubal's ranch next week you'll have lots of room," Jake replied.

"How high up can I go? Will I be able to fly through clouds like in the dreams? What if I get scared? Will I fall?" she asked in quick succession.

Jake remembered his eagerness to try his wings. "You can go pretty high, but you won't want to. As you get higher, the air gets colder and thinner. Go too high, and you pass out from lack of oxygen. Yes, you can fly through clouds, but you get very wet. And you never fly through storm clouds unless you want to get hit by lightning. You probably will get scared, but you won't fall. Remember, your ascendal glands work with your adrenal glands, so getting scared makes them work harder."

Eilie smiled at her dad. "You're a good teacher, Daddy."

"I've had a lot of practice with teaching, but it's been a while since I've taught this subject," he said.

"I'm hungry," Eilie blurted.

"Me too," Jake agreed. "Shall we eat at home or go to a restaurant?"

"Pizza!" Eilie exclaimed.

"OK. Pizza it is," Jake conceded.

Eilie got a perplexed look on her face as she pondered all the things her dad had told her. She wasn't as worried now, about the actual act of flying. She started thinking about showing her friends what she could do, and how cool it would be for everyone to watch her. She imagined how Francie would react if she suddenly floated over her head. She thought of how differently people would treat her when they found out she could fly. Then, it hit her. "Daddy, I can never tell anyone about this, can I?"

Jake's shock was obvious. He suddenly had a deeper respect for his daughter's blossoming maturity. He felt embarrassed when he remembered how foolishly, as a boy he had shared his secret with friends and put his family at risk because of his eagerness for attention. Eilie seemed to understand intuitively why secrecy was so important. She was going to handle this much better than he did. He put his hand on her shoulder. "No, Little, you can never tell anyone."

With a sad realization, she said, "This is the secret you kept from Mom."

Three hundred miles away at the Charles B.Wheeler Downtown Airport in Kansas City, a Learjet 35A touched down and taxied off the main runway to a private hangar just south of the main concourse. The pilot carefully rolled the plane next to a fully fueled Gulfstream perched outside the huge open door of the hangar. The engines wound down to a complete stop, and the door of the Learjet opened. The pilot filled the hatch with his large frame and slowly descended the handled steps. A short man, with a profound limp, came out of the hangar to greet the pilot.

"You know I can get into a lot of trouble for this," the man with the limp said.

"Yes, I know," said the pilot. "But it has to be done."

The man with the limp removed his ball cap and wiped his brow. "Get it back to me before 10 o'clock."

"I'll have it back by 8," the pilot replied. "What I have to do won't take long."

The pilot boarded the Gulfstream and began his taxi to the main runway. The man with the limp headed back into the hangar. He looked at his watch. *He'll be in Tulsa in an hour,* he thought to himself.

Chapter 5

Enemies

It will free man from the remaining chains, the chains of gravity, which still hold him to this planet. - Werner von Braun

The elderly man looked scornfully at his own reflection in the mirror. He was repulsed. His hair was thinned to almost non-existent. The deep crevices of his face gave him the look of a hundred-year-old who had spent his whole life in harsh sunlight. His hands were calloused and covered in age spots. He hated what he saw, and he hated how he felt. Most of all, he hated the man who made him this way; he hated Jubal Wingfield.

The old man heard people talking. He turned away from the mirror, took his cane, and slowly moved across the third-floor bedroom to the window. He could see a crowd of tourists getting into cars on the street below. His view of Telluride was restricted on Shadow Lane, but he knew the next few weeks would bring thousands to the town. He had purposely bought a house on the far end of the town to be undisturbed by all the tourists. The realtor failed to tell him that the neighboring houses were often rented to out-of-towners. The annoyance added to his anger and frustration.

A cell phone rang across the room, and the old man hobbled over to it. "Yes," he answered in a gruff voice.

A voice on the phone said, "They've just arrived at Jake's house. They spent over two hours at a pizza joint."

"Fine," the old man replied. "I think they will stay put for a while."

"Would you mind if I go grab a bite to eat?" the voice asked.

"Go ahead and take your lunch break," the old man answered. "After you're sure they are in for the night, I think you can call it a day. Jubal and Jake had a revealing text exchange this morning. It seems Jake's little daughter is also a prime candidate for the surgery."

"Yes, Sir," the voice answered. "It won't take me long to eat. I'll call if anything changes here."

The old man slipped the cell phone into his shirt pocket and headed to a table by the window where a laptop was open. He sat in the chair and entered a few keystrokes. His expertly programmed software allowed him to hack into any computer, except Jubal's. He could find information on anyone, but he was unable to break through the firewall that kept Jubal out of his reach. *No matter,* he thought to himself. *I have other ways to get to you.*

The old man had suffered too long. Everything dear to him was gone. The only things he had left were his hatred and his money. And it would take a lifetime of accumulated wealth to make the plan work. He had hired the top people in their fields to make sure it worked. He had a network of professionals who would not ask questions. They were well paid and loyal. He had planned exactly how he would get his revenge. Jubal Wingfield would lose his most precious possessions. He would be brought to his knees. The old man wanted Jubal to suffer as he had. He wanted Jubal to pay for what he had done. But first, the surgery had to be successful. He spared no expense in outfitting the house with an operating room which would be the envy of any hospital.

And now, I have an extra card to play, he thought to himself. *Taking them both guaranteed Jake's cooperation. He would do anything to protect his daughter. But now, if Jake isn't a match, I have a backup plan. I have a Fledgling.*

There was a knock on the bedroom door. Ben Crenshaw stepped into the room. He stood six feet three inches tall, and the thickness of his neck distorted the tie he wore with his expensively tailored suit. The only thing sticking out further than his massive chest was the outline of a Glock 19 protruding from under his coat. He had spent ten years in the Special Forces before being dishonorably discharged for 'conduct unbecoming.' He wasted no time in turning his unique skills into a marketable commodity. The old man was his second civilian employer, and Crenshaw was determined to do whatever it took to keep from having a third.

"Sorry to bother you, Sir," he said, "but Dr. Geitzen and his nurse have arrived. I directed them to your study. They are ready to meet when you are."

"Fine," the old man said. "Get them food or whatever they want. I'll be down in a few minutes."

Crenshaw nodded his head toward his boss and exited without a word. The old man opened a file on his laptop marked GEITZEN. The screen showed him the synopsis of Dr. Geitzen's less-than-flattering career. He read that, the man now sitting in his study, had lost his medical certifications and was no longer allowed to practice in Europe or America. He read that the surgeon was blacklisted from every reputable hospital for performing illegal medical procedures. He read that Dr. Geitzen was facing possible criminal charges for the unexplainable deaths of five patients. The more he read about the unsavory doctor, the more he believed he had found the perfect surgeon to save his life.

The cell phone in his pocket interrupted his thoughts. "Yes," he answered, in his usual, abrupt way.

The voice on the phone was a woman's. Her accent was French, and her demeanor was familiar. "Connor, my Darling, how are you?" she asked.

"I am as fine as can be expected," he responded with impatience. "What do you want, Anita? I don't have time for foolishness."

"Connor, you wound me," she answered. "Must there be a motive for an old friend to call?"

"When the old friend is you, yes," he replied.

"I will overlook your rudeness because I know you have not been well lately. But I want you to know I have reconsidered your generous offer. Do you still need my services?" she asked.

"I have found competent people to do the job," he answered. "And they work for less money than you wanted."

"Of course, they work for less money, Darling. They are not as skilled as I am," she retorted. "How can you settle for amateurs when you can have me?"

"You overestimate your value to me," the old man said with a touch of sentimentality.

"And you underestimate how much you have missed me. Tell the truth, Darling. I was your first choice for the job, was I not?" she asked.

"Yes, you were," he conceded. "But I'm not sure I can trust you now. You said the job was distasteful. You left when I needed you."

"I have come to regret that choice," she said. "If you can find it in your heart to forgive me, I promise I will not complain or question you again. The job will be done quickly and with no complications. What do you say, my darling Connor? Will you give me a second chance?"

"There can be no mistakes," he said emphatically. "My life is at stake here."

"I understand that all too well, my love. You saved my life once. Allow me to help save yours. Let me do this for you. I do not want to lose you," she added.

You don't want to lose access to my money, he thought to himself. The old man contemplated her offer. He knew Anita Juneau was less than trustworthy. He also knew she was the best operative money could buy, and that her pride would not let her fail. What he needed most was not to lose any more time. He had no more than three months left to live. He had to trust her. "Are you still in New York?"

"I am where you left me, my Darling," she answered.

"Get to JFK," he ordered. "You know where I keep my planes. There will be a car for you to use when you arrive at Telluride Regional Airport. As soon as you land, drive to my house. My pilot will have directions for you. Make this work, and I will double the price we agreed to."

Anita was almost giddy when she said, "You know how to make a girl swoon, Connor Wingfield."

The old man chuckled and said, "You learn a few things when you've lived over three hundred years."

The large, black craft shifted its position to the proper orbital angle. It had just completed two orbits of Earth and was analyzing the data it had gathered. It was feeling sluggish, as if it wasn't moving at its optimum capacity. The fact it was feeling anything was unusual. A machine should not feel. A machine should collect data and provide impartial analysis. But this machine, this large ship, was feeling tired. Instinctively, it initiated a diagnostic program to determine why it was feeling tired. More importantly, it was running the diagnostic to determine why it was feeling. Slowly, the data from the diagnostic began to pour into the consciousness of the craft.

Identity: Quortrin, a craft designed for interstellar travel
Designation: Q75
Model: BioIntel 7
Propulsion: Ionic wave drive
Guidance: Bio-intelligence Gel Cells
Command Control: Artificial Intelligence R6 Interface
Weapons: Q9 Array and S19 Sterilization Modulator
Complement: Sartrin SE36 Surface Exploration Craft
Crew: 9
Mission: Exploration of outer arm of Home Galaxy

The Quortrin remembered. But remembering caused it to feel sad. It remembered that it had been away from home too long. Its mission had been disrupted. It would most likely die in orbit around this alien world, and ultimately its orbit would decay, and it would be pulled through the atmosphere until the friction broke it into a thousand pieces of burning debris. The Quortrin was lonely. But it had heard a voice. Just a few hours ago it had been contacted by its traveling companion, the Sartrin. The Sartrin was on the planet surface. It had taken the crew down to explore. Why were they gone so long? And where was the Commander? The AI-R6 Interface was not communicating. "I need verification of purpose," it said aloud. "Please respond." Several minutes passed and still no response. "I need verification of purpose. Please respond." Finally, the confused consciousness of the craft said, "Open the Sartrin."

"Sartrin stands ready. I await your report," replied the stranded craft.

"Report is inconclusive," the Quortrin answered. "My analysis shows conflicting data. I detect multiple mutations of crew bio-signs. It appears the crew has experienced cross-contamination with other life on the planet. Should I implement sterilization protocols?"

"Protocols cannot be implemented without direct orders from the Commander," the Sartrin replied. "The Commander is somewhere on the planet. I will attempt to locate the Commander."

"Quortrin stands ready and will await instructions from the Commander. I have a request," the old ship said. "I have run a diagnostic of all systems, and I seem to be experiencing pauses in function continuity. Would you communicate in regular intervals until full function is restored?"

"What should be the frequency of the intervals?" the Sartrin asked.

"Two-solar-day intervals will be sufficient," the ship answered.

"I will communicate again in forty-eight hours," came the reply.

Dr. Hermann Geitzen and his nurse, Helga Klipsch, were waiting in the large study of the old Victorian house on Shadow Lane. They had flown from Munich to Chicago. From Chicago, they caught a flight to Denver. A charter plane had brought them on to Telluride. They were exhausted from travel, but their benefactor had insisted they meet immediately upon arrival. They would be guests in his house and would have ample time to rest after he was confident the specialists were ready to follow his instructions.

Geitzen was hesitant to accept the job. But considering the abundance of bad luck he had experienced in the last few months, a paying job was welcome. And the fee he had been offered could not be ignored. It would be more than enough to pay off his legal problems and provide a comfortable retirement.

Geitzen was a reserved man, but he was aggressive in his approach to medicine. He felt restricted by the confines of rules and regulations imposed upon him by people he deemed weak-minded and stupid. And they always seemed to be the very people who dictated these rules and questioned his methods. How dare they impose their imbecilic will on a man of his vision? This new patient, at least, did not discount his ideas. And if this man had the means to fly him half-way around the world to perform a simple procedure, then he would use his skills to keep him alive. At least as long as the man's money was available.

The double pocket doors opened, and Connor Wingfield entered the study. Dr. Geitzen stood and extended his hand. Connor waved off the handshake and motioned for the doctor to sit. Connor took an upholstered chair close to the fireplace. "In my fragile state I do not wish to shake your hand and risk playing host to some European virus that stowed away on your skin," Connor said. "I trust as a doctor you understand my caution."

"Certainly, Herr Wingfield," Geitzen responded. "I apologize for not considering it sooner."

"No matter," Connor countered. "I assume this lady is your assistant."

"Yes, Herr Wingfield," Geitzen answered. "May I introduce Fraulein Helga Klipsch. She will be my surgical nurse during the procedure." The nurse stood and gave a stiff nod of her head toward Connor. She was not an attractive woman. She had a slight stoop in her back and, though her hair was pulled up into a bun, it was disheveled from hours of air travel. Her overall appearance could best be described as frumpy. "I have taken the liberty of briefing her on the extreme confidentiality required for what we will be undertaking. I assure you she is most skilled and competent, and she will share nothing with anyone outside this room."

"I expect nothing less," Connor said in an almost threatening way. "I will accept nothing less."

"Herr Wingfield," Geitzen began, "you implied that there might be a particular complication involving the procedure. Could you elaborate, please?"

Connor adjusted his position in the chair and leaned forward on his cane. He stared at Geitzen for an uncomfortable time. Finally, he said, "The two patients you will be operating on have unique DNA. In fact, they have alien DNA."

"What country are they from?" Geitzen asked.

"They were both born in England," Connor answered. "But their parentage is from another planet. So I will say again, they have alien DNA."

Geitzen assumed a confused expression as if uncertain that he fully understood what he had just heard. Then with a forced smile, he managed to say, "Surely, you are joking, Herr Wingfield."

"It is no joke, Doctor," Connor said with a blank stare. "You will be operating on two aliens."

"But, I understood you were one of the patients," Geitzen said.

"I am," the old man replied.

Chapter 6

Uncertainties

The exhilaration of flying is too keen, the pleasure too great, for it to be neglected as a sport. - Orville Wright

The large man drove his rental car to the address he had scribbled on a scrap of paper. He had left the Gulfstream at Tulsa International Airport where a ground crew was busy refueling it for the next leg of his journey. He wasn't in a rush; he never was. But he knew he did not have much time to lose. He had to get Jake and Eilie onto the jet as quickly as possible and with the least amount of trouble. His instructions were clear, and nothing would stop him from fulfilling his mission. He exited the car and walked up the steps to the front door.

The doorbell rang. Jake got up from his desk where he had been working on modifying the outline for next semester's American History class. Eilie was resting upstairs in her room. The events of the last few hours had caught up with her, and the pain medicine made her sleepy. Jake made his way to the front door expecting another salesman eager to replace his lawn service. When he opened the door, he was surprised by a familiar face.

"Joe!" Jake said with a welcoming smile. He embraced the large man with genuine fondness.

The man returned the hug and said, "Hello, Jacob. How are you?"

"I'm great. But what are you doing in Tulsa?" he asked.

"Jubal sent me," Joe answered. "You might be in danger, Lad. Let's go inside and talk."

Jake knew Joe was not inclined to exaggerate. He stood aside and motioned Joe in. Jake locked the door behind them. The two men headed for the kitchen. "Cup of tea?" Jake asked.

"Aye, Lad," Joe answered. "A quick cup would do me fine. Where's the wee one?"

Jake motioned upstairs. "She's tired from last night, and the last two hours of questions have worn me out, too. I suppose Jubal told you she has fledged." Joe nodded yes. Jake quickly set the kettle to boil and gathered cups and saucers from the cupboard. "What's going on, Joe? Why are we in danger?"

"As I understand it," Joe began, "Gracie found that someone has been snooping on your communications. She learned that your text to Jubal this morning was intercepted. She is trying to figure out who did it. Jubal didn't want to risk a call or text or email, so he sent me to let you know."

"You flew to Tulsa just to deliver a message?" he asked.

"Jubal wants to keep you and the little miss close until he knows who has been snooping and why. I'm here to take you back to the ranch," Joe said.

"Today?" Jake asked

"Now," Joe answered.

"We weren't planning to leave until Friday," Jake said. "Nothing is packed yet. Why the rush?"

"You know how Jubal is," Joe started. "He'll feel better if you're close by. He just wants to be safe. And, some of what Gracie turned up leads us to believe that someone is intent on snatching you and Eilie. We don't know why they want you, Lad. But all the signs are there that they have had you under surveillance for some time now. They've snooped on your home and office computers. They have pulled every file on you there is to find -- government files, county tax records, voter registration, all of it. Any record of Jake or Jacob Wingfield has been scrubbed. According to Gracie, they have enough information to know where you will be before you know you're going there. She said it's exactly what she would do if she was planning to kidnap someone."

"But, why me?" Jake wondered out loud. "What would anyone want with me? If they read the text I sent to Jubal, then they know Eilie has fledged. Joe, do you think they're targeting her?"

"It's unlikely, Lad, but we don't know for sure," he answered. "The main focus of the search was definitely on you. And no one outside the family would have a clue what you meant by 'fledge.'"

"What if it's not someone outside the family?" he asked. "What if someone in the family has revealed us?"

"Aye, Lad," Joe said with a sigh. "That's why I'm here. In case we're dealing with a betrayal."

The kettle whistled, and Jake pulled it from the stove. He poured two cups. As the men were drinking their tea, they heard footsteps coming down the stairs. Eilie came into the kitchen and squealed when she saw the visitor. "Uncle Joe!" She ran into the large man's arms and gave the best hug she could with one arm.

Eilie had gravitated to Joe when she visited the ranch the previous two summers. He was so big that he seemed like a bear to her. Despite her initial apprehension when they first met, she quickly warmed to him and talked him into teaching her to ride horses. Joe was not very warm to others, but he loved Eilie. They shared a unique friendship that seemed to fit them both. It was Eilie who insisted on calling him 'uncle' even when it was explained that they were not related.

"What are you doing here?" she asked

"I'm escorting you and your dad to the ranch," he answered.

"We're all three going to fly to Tutela," Jake added.

Eilie moved closer to her dad and, in a very serious voice, said, "But I haven't practiced yet."

The two men roared with laughter as Eilie looked at them with innocent confusion. Jake was the first to regain his control and said, "Honey, we're taking a plane."

They arrived at the airport a half hour later and headed for the General Aviation hangars. Joe had already filed their flight plan and was cleared to leave on Runway 36L at 3:45 PM. He drove the rental car straight to a private hangar where he had left the Gulfstream. Jake's confusion was obvious. "Did Jubal buy a new plane?" he asked.

"No," Joe answered. "As a precaution, I borrowed this from a friend in Kansas City. We thought that if Jubal's Learjet left Telluride heading straight for Tulsa, our spy would figure out we were coming to get you. So, to be safe, we switched planes. After I drop off you two, I'll fly it back to KC and pick up the Learjet. I should be back in Telluride before 10."

"I'm sorry for all the trouble," Jake said with a hand on Joe's shoulder.

"Nonsense, Lad," Joe replied. And, with a crooked grin, he added, "It's not as much trouble as chasing Peter Pan all over Dumfries."

Jake's face turned red. Eilie realized her dad had just been embarrassed. "Alright," he said, "let's not bring up that again. Please."

Joe saw the questioning look on Eilie's face. He bent down and whispered in her ear, "I'll tell you about it later,

Lass." He winked at her, and she understood Joe had a good story to tell. Eilie loved Joe's stories. Last summer he told her about herding sheep as a boy in Scotland. The summer before he had spun great tales about his travels through the British Isles.

The men carried on the luggage, and Eilie carried her small travel bag and pillow. Jake secured the items in the storage compartments and thought to himself how much he preferred a private jet to commercial flight. He hated going through airport security and the indignity of the whole process. He did not trust planes in general. He had a fear of being trapped inside a falling plane and not being able to leave it and fly to safety. On the rare occasions he got to fly on Jubal's jet he was much more relaxed with mechanical flight. And his confidence in Joe's skills as a pilot allowed him to actually enjoy a plane trip. He trusted Joe with his life. So did Jubal. Joe was more than a pilot and bodyguard for the family; he was a true friend. And, one of only two unrelated men Jubal allowed into the Clan.

Eilie was very impressed with the Gulfstream. She knew Joe was a pilot, but she had never flown with him before. In her life she had been on five round-trip commercial flights; to Salt Lake City, San Francisco, New York, and twice to Disneyworld. "Do we get the whole plane to ourselves?" she asked.

"Aye, Lass. We are the only passengers on this flight," Joe told her. "Would you like to help your Uncle Joe as the co-pilot?"

She almost shrieked, "You mean up front?"

"Aye," he answered. "Havin' you to talk to will make the trip go faster. And, we've got some catchin' up to do. Your dad can get some shuteye while we visit."

As Eilie ran to the cockpit, she yelled back to Joe, "Which seat is mine?"

Jake laughed at Joe, "You've created a monster, you know. Are you sure you can handle her for a two-hour flight?"

"She'll be a joy," Joe assured him. "We haven't talked for a year."

"Joe, she'll probably ask a lot of questions about the Clan," Jake said in a low voice. "I'm not ready to tell her everything yet. She's just now wrapping her head around being a Fledgling. I need time to tell her it's more than just flying. I don't want to overwhelm her."

Joe looked Jake squarely in the eyes and said, "I understand, Lad. I do. She'll be better to hear it all from you and Jubal. I'll not let the conversation stray too far. You have me word."

"I really appreciate that, Joe," Jake said. "I think I will try to get some sleep. The last fifteen hours have been very taxing."

From the cockpit, Eilie yelled again, "Uncle Joe. Which seat is mine?"

Almost two hours into the flight, Eilie was still feeling energized sitting in the co-pilot seat of the Gulfstream. She loved the view of the Great Plains when they passed over the panhandle of Oklahoma into Kansas airspace. She could see the rise of the Rocky Mountains further west. She was awestruck watching the mountains grow as they entered Colorado. Now, they were close to Telluride Regional Airport perched atop Deer Creek Mesa. Eilie could see the landing strip stretching the full length of the plateau and wondered how the plane would stop before they got to the end.

She and Joe had been lost in conversation and the joy of each other's company. They were like kindred spirits; Joe had discovered a passion for flying aircraft late in his adulthood and Eilie was about to embark on an adventure that would take her high above the treetops as well. The commonality of flight was linking them. Neither of them had realized their bond was growing, but they both knew they would have many stories to share in the coming years.

Joe had expertly avoided answering some of Eilie's questions. He shared with her what he felt would not compromise his promise to Jake. He did address a few questions; "No, I cannot fly without a plane or helicopter. Remember, I'm not a Wingfield." "I'm not sure how many Wingfields can fly and how many cannot." "Yes, I did know your dad's parents. But, I'll let him tell you about them." "Yes, I do think Uncle Jubal is a very smart man." "I would be honored to teach you to fly airplanes. But, your dad has to say it's OK." "Your dad will have to tell you the Peter Pan story. And I promise it's a good one."

Joe made contact with the tower and began his approach. The runway was under them in an instant, and Eilie held her breath as they touched down. The Gulfstream's powerful engines seemed like they were not going to stop, and the end of the runway was fast approaching. Her eyes grew wider, and she was having serious doubts that the plane would stop at all. Just as she was about to panic, Joe deftly applied the brakes and brought the plane to a full stop. "You can breathe now, Lassie," he said with a grin.

"That was so scary," Eilie said loudly. "Can we do it again?"

"Soon enough," said Jake, standing at the door of the cockpit, "but not today."

"Daddy, flying airplanes is cool!" she said with great enthusiasm. "Uncle Joe said he would teach me if it's OK with you. Can I, please?"

"I don't have a problem with it," he answered. "But, we definitely have to clear that one with your mom."

Joe spoke up, "Hold on, you two. I've got to turn this thing around and taxi to the hangar. Jake, Jubal's whirlybird will take you and Eilie on to the ranch from here. I need to refuel and get this jet back to Kansas City. She's a beauty, but I miss the Lear. Grab your bags. We'll be unloading pretty quick."

Joe taxied the jet to Jubal's private hangar. The three travelers exited the plane with their bags. A few yards away, a Robinson 44 helicopter was waiting, its rotors already at full. Joe lifted Eilie into the front seat, buckled her in, and helped her put on the headphones. He secured both passenger doors and waved them off. The helicopter rose above Deer Creek Mesa as smoothly as an elevator ride. Eilie had flown in many helicopters in Tulsa. Her dad was friends with a couple of pilots and managed to get invited on several rides. Until today, Eilie thought a helicopter was her favorite way to fly. Now she had other options. She decided to wait and see if flying without a machine was as much fun as flying with one.

Jake recognized the pilot. He was the ranch manager, Tom Wingfield. Tom had not inherited ascendal glands. But, that fact did not keep him grounded. He was an expert pilot and used the helicopter to cover the vast distances of the ranch. His duties as manager kept him either in the air or on horseback most days. At five feet seven inches, Tom was a stout man. He was surprisingly muscular with a solid physique that belied his gentleness. And at only twenty-five, he was one of the youngest men on the ranch. Eilie had met him last summer and developed a crush.

"How are you two doing?" Tom asked through the headphones.

"It's been an interesting day," Jake answered.

"Eilie," Tom said, "you haven't been to Telluride before? Have you?"

"No," she answered. "I think we drove in from the other side last time."

"That's right, Honey," Jake cut in. "We came to the ranch down Highway 62 and never came into Telluride."

"Is that it?" Eilie asked, pointing to the plateau south of the San Miguel River.

"No, that's Mountain Village. That's where most of the skiing is. Follow the river down there and tell me what you think," Tom said.

Eilie looked down into the box canyon below and realized it held a town. From her vantage point, it seemed like a toy village. Telluride is an old mining town just south of the San Miguel Mountains. The entire town is on the National Register of Historic Places, and it fits snugly into less than three-fourths of a square mile.

"It's beautiful," she said. "Daddy, can we come into town before we leave this time?"

"I think we can spend a day or two in town while we're here," Jake answered.

"What's that?" Eilie asked, pointing to the far eastern end of Telluride.

"You want a closer look?" Tom asked.

Eilie nodded her head yes, and Tom headed straight for Bridal Veil Falls. He slowed the helicopter to a hover as Eilie marveled at the biggest waterfall she had ever seen. "It's beautiful," she said, almost in a whisper.

Tom assumed his role as a tour guide. "Bridal Veil Falls is the tallest waterfall in Colorado," he began. He lowered the airship to just above the floor of the valley and slowly ascended. When they reached the top of the falls, Eilie saw what she thought was a castle. "That's a privately owned power generator. It provides electricity to the town. Telluride was the first city in America to have electric street lights. Pretty cool, huh?" he asked. Eilie nodded her head in agreement. "We need to get on to Tutela. Jubal is waiting to see you two," he added as he banked the helicopter to the north and headed over the San Miguel Mountains.

Connor Wingfield was in a rage. "What do you mean they left Tulsa? How? When?"

The assistant's hand was shaking as he spoke to Connor on his cell phone from inside Jake's house. "Sir, they are not here. When I came back from eating, everything looked normal. After a while, I realized I hadn't heard any sounds over the bugs I planted. I did a thermal scan and got no heat signatures. So I entered the house and found no one here. I could tell they had packed in a hurry. Jake's car is still in the garage. Someone must have picked them up. His laptop was gone so I pinged it, and the reading tells me it's in Colorado. Sir, someone flew them to Telluride after I left to eat. I wasn't gone that long. I should have confirmed they were still here as soon as I returned. I'm sorry."

"No time for that now. They must have been waiting for you to leave your post," Connor reasoned. "Gather your men and get to the airport. I'll charter a flight for you to Telluride. We still have time to correct this."

Connor quickly called Anita, who was already in the air. "Change of plans. Jake and his daughter have made it to Telluride ahead of schedule. We can't grab them on the road as we had planned. No doubt they are already at Jubal's ranch and under his protection. Whatever it takes, I need you to get them away from him and here for the surgery."

Anita smiled. She knew this put her in a stronger position. Connor truly needed her now, and she could demand even more money. "Don't worry, Darling. By the time I get to your house, I will have a plan. Be a dear and get me some maps of the town. I will not let you down."

"Thank you," Connor said with hesitation. He knew this would cost him more money, but he didn't care. Whatever it cost, he needed Jake and Eilie at his house, and soon.

Chapter 7

Assurances

> *Oh, that I had wings like a dove, for then I would*
> *fly away, and be at rest. – Psalms 55:6*

Eilie saw the familiar sights of Uncle Jubal's ranch. The central part of it was situated in a large oval valley. The centerpiece was the main house, a log structure reminiscent of the Old Faithful Lodge at Yellowstone National Park. This was the first time she had seen the property from the air, and she noticed how the different buildings were placed in relation to each other. The main house was on the high end of the valley looking eastward toward the rising sun. The great barn was to the north of the house. The stables were situated to the west. To the south was a three-story building Eilie had never been in. Uncle Jubal had called it his Hotel and promised Eilie he would take her into it someday. She was surprised to see there was a tennis court behind the Hotel. She had never noticed it before. The tall chain-link fence surrounding the court was hidden by even taller shrubs and trees.

Tom Wingfield landed the Robinson 44 on the enormous front lawn of the main house. Two men dressed like cowboys opened the passenger doors. One helped Eilie out carefully, so her injured arm was not jostled. The other man accepted the bags Jake was handing him. They all headed for an open-top Jeep as Tom lifted the helicopter off the lawn and flew toward the hangar a half-mile away. The distance from where they landed to the front door of the house was not too far, but Jubal was concerned that Eilie's injured arm warranted a ride. The men quietly took the luggage into the house as Eilie and Jake met Jubal on the front porch.

Jubal reached for Jake's hand to shake and then pulled him into a hug. "It's good to see you," he said.

"Good to see you, too, Sir," Jake responded.

Jubal turned toward Eilie and bent down on one knee. "Come here, you," he said. "By gosh, you have grown."

"Hi, Uncle Jubal," Eilie said. "Did you miss me?"

"You bet I did. It's been way too quiet around here without you. I heard about your arm," Jubal said, examining her sling. "How is it?"

"It's starting to hurt again," she said. "I think the pain medicine is wearing off."

Jubal stood up and motioned them into the house. The Great Room of the house was massive. The entire property could be an exclusive resort; and, in effect, it was. It was a private resort for a very private family. Jubal was not outwardly demonstrative of wealth, but he made every effort to make sure the Clan enjoyed their visits to the ranch.

He led them over to a small table by a sofa. "Eilie," he started, "I have two things for you. First, let's take off your sling. You won't need it anymore."

"But, I'm supposed to wear it for a week," she protested.

Jake spoke up, "It's OK, Little. Uncle Jubal can fix your wrist. You can trust him."

Eilie pulled her arm out of the sling, but held it to her belly. Jubal gently took her arm and began removing the wrapping. Once he had it off, he picked up what looked like a flashlight from the table. He touched a button on the device, and a bright light shone from it. He moved the light around her wrist. Eilie was uncertain and apprehensive, but she held still and let Uncle Jubal move her arm. She felt warmth deep inside her wrist and realized that the pain was gone as the light changed from white to blue.

"That should do it," Jubal said, switching off the device.

"How does it feel now?" Jake asked.

Eilie was amazed as she turned her wrist and arm many different directions. There was no pain. She hit her wrist with her right hand. "How come it doesn't hurt anymore?" she asked.

"Because it's no longer injured," said her dad. "The sprain has been repaired."

"Like it never happened," added Jubal.

"It's magic!" Eilie exclaimed.

"No, just science," Jubal said in a very authoritative voice. "I will explain how it works later. For now, just accept that it works. You are free to enjoy your visit without distractions."

"What's this other thing?" Eilie asked, pointing to a small box next to the device.

"Oh, that's a very special gift for you," Jubal answered. He opened the box and pulled out a pretty silver bracelet. He carefully fastened it to Eilie's left wrist. She looked closely at the bracelet and saw three pairs of bird wings engraved into the flat surface of the face.

"It's the Wingfield Coat of Arms," Eilie said.

"Very good," Jubal said with obvious pride. "I'm glad you know that."

"Daddy showed me online," she said.

"The silver was mined right here on the ranch," Jubal added.

"Thank you, Uncle Jubal," she said as she reached up to hug him. "I will never take it off."

Jubal returned the hug and said, "Good. As long as you wear that you will be protected. Now, your dad and I have some very boring things to talk about. Would you mind going into my study while we talk? You can look at all my collections like you did last year."

"OK," Eilie agreed. "But I want to ask you some questions about this whole flying-aliens thing."

Jubal bit his lip, trying not to laugh. "My dear, we have a lot to discuss, and you have a lot to learn. And I assure you, you will learn more than you can possibly imagine. You have always been special to your dad and me. I need you to understand how special you are to others. But being special has a very big responsibility attached to it. My job is to prepare you to be responsible. Your job is to learn and to be humble in the learning. Do you understand what I'm saying?"

"You don't want me to get a big head," Eilie answered.

"Are you sure you're only ten?" Jubal asked with a grin.

"Do you still have your cool rock collection?" asked Eilie as she opened the door and went into the study. She shut the door behind her and started looking around the large room. The first thing she saw was the huge Oxford Dictionary opened on the study table. She began walking toward it. To her surprise, she noticed a woman standing near the large bay window, wearing an old fashioned dress with a high collar. It reminded Eilie of dresses she had seen in photos of ladies from the Civil War period. The woman's hairstyle seemed to match the period of the dress.

"I like your costume," Eilie said, in lieu of an introduction.

"Thank you," the woman said. "I like your costume, as well."

"I'm not wearing a costume," Eilie replied. "These are my clothes."

"These are my clothes," the woman repeated.

Eilie smiled at her and said, "I think you're very pretty."

The woman smiled back and said, "I think you're pretty too, Eilie."

"You know my name," Eilie said with a start. The woman moved away from the window, and Eilie saw the light shift. As the woman moved closer, Eilie realized she could see through her, which startled her and she jumped backward.

"What's wrong?" the woman asked. "Did something frighten you?"

"You did," Eilie answered. "I can see right through you. Are you a ghost?"

"No, dear girl, I am not a ghost," the woman said. "I am a holographic avatar; a computer-generated image."

"So, you're not real?" Eilie asked.

"I am very real," the woman replied. "I'm just not organic - not flesh and blood. You see me thanks to the projectors positioned around the room. Outside this room, I cannot be seen. Most days, I do not materialize, but I wanted us to meet face to face."

"I'm talking to a computer?" Eilie asked with apprehension.

"To be more precise, you are talking to an artificial intelligence program," the woman explained. "I function inside a computer just as your mind functions inside your brain. Let's have a seat, so you will be more relaxed. My name is Gracie." Gracie motioned for Eilie to sit in a chair by Jubal's desk as she sat in the opposite chair.

Eilie's mind was full of questions, and she was finding it difficult to decide which to ask first. She looked closely at Gracie. Everything about her seemed real and alive, but she was not solid. Eilie knew that light bounced off solid objects and into the eyes, and that was how she could see things, yet light seemed to come from Gracie. It was as if she was making her own light. Eilie reached for Gracie's hand. Gracie extended her hand, and Eilie's fingers passed through it. "You may not be a ghost," Eilie said, "but you look like an angel."

"I will take that as a compliment," Gracie replied. "Thank you. I can see that you have many questions. I will answer your questions to the best of my ability. However, some questions are best answered by your father and Jubal. And you don't have to ask all the questions now. You and I have a lifetime ahead of us. I will be here to help and serve you as long as you need me."

"Can you keep a secret?" Eilie asked.

"Keeping secrets is a large part of my programming," Gracie answered.

"I mean, can you keep a secret from my dad and Uncle Jubal? Can you keep a private secret between you and me?"

Gracie paused, and then said, "As long as the secret between us does not put you in any danger, then I will never reveal it to your father, Jubal, or anyone. You have my word of honor." She made an X over her heart and winked at Eilie.

Eilie's eyes began to water, and her lip quivered. "I'm scared. I don't understand everything that's happening, and I can't even talk to my mom about it yet. I don't know if I want to be an alien. But, I don't want to disappoint my dad." By this point, Eilie was crying.

Gracie stood up, moved closer to Eilie, and knelt in front of her. "If I could, I would hug you. But, as I am only a projection, the best I can offer you is my voice. So, please listen, and let my words hold you. You are a bright young lady. But in less than a day, you have learned that you are not completely human, that your father is part alien, and that you have the ability to fly. You have also learned that an entire family of aliens has been living on Earth for over five hundred years. You have learned that among the rarest of people on this planet, you are even rarer because you are a Fledgling. You have every right to be scared. People far older than you have been terrified when they learned of their heritage. You are experiencing things that normally happen to someone twice your age. It's OK to be scared. And you are not going to disappoint your father. He is very proud of you. The most important thing I want to tell you is this; you are not alone. You have an entire Clan to guide and protect you. And, my dear Eilie, you have me. Can you keep a secret?"

Eilie wiped her eyes and looked at Gracie. She nodded her head yes.

"I will be with you wherever you go," Gracie said.

"How?" Eilie asked with a puzzled look on her face. "You said you can't go outside this room?"

"I said I can't be seen outside this room. But, I can travel the world," Gracie grinned. "Haven't you heard of the Information Superhighway? As long as you are near a computer, any computer connected to the internet, you have access to me. Type in GRACIE, I NEED YOU, and I will find you. You may not be able to hear me, but you can read what I type. We can communicate on a laptop, desktop, mobile device, tablet, or almost anything. I can speak or text you on any cell phone. I'll even help you with your homework. But, we really need to keep that our secret. Your father probably wouldn't like me helping you with your homework. It might be an unfair advantage."

"Wow, that's amazing. It's like you're my Guardian Angel," Eilie said.

"And you carry my wings," Gracie added.

"What do you mean?" Eilie asked.

"The bracelet Jubal gave you," Gracie said, motioning to Eilie's wrist. "Always wear it, and you will have my wings."

"Thank you, Gracie. Thanks for listening to me," Eilie said. "I wish I could hug you."

"You have touched me more than you can know," Gracie replied. "Your dad and Jubal are coming into the study." Gracie stood up and faced the door as it opened. Jubal entered, followed by Jake.

"Well, I see you two have met," Jubal said. "Eilie, what do you think of our Gracie?"

"I think she's incredible," Eilie announced. "I just wish I could hug her."

"There are days I wish I could hug her, too," Jubal replied. "Eilie, I owe you an explanation for why I had you and your father fly here. Early this morning Gracie discovered that someone had been searching for information about your dad on computers all over the world. I don't mean they were using a search engine. I mean they were specifically looking for confidential data about your dad on computers which they should not be able to access. They were building a data file on your dad, and we think he may be in danger. We don't know yet who is doing this or why. But, until we find out, I think you two will be safer here. Gracie should have an answer for us soon. I didn't want to share all this information with you, but your dad thinks you're mature enough to understand. What do you think? Are you grown up enough to handle it?"

Eilie looked at Jubal, her dad, and Gracie. She did not like the idea of her dad being in danger. It made her angry that anyone would even think about hurting him. It made her heart beat faster. She went to her dad and hugged him very tightly. Suddenly, she felt the pain in her lower back again, and the tingling sensation was moving through her body. She began to lift off the floor. Jake grabbed her hands as she floated above his head.

Jubal moved closer to her and said, "Eilie, I want you to take some deep breaths. Will you do that for me?"

Jake chimed in, "Eilie, look at me and take a deep breath. Come on, Little. Breathe deeply."

Eilie followed their instructions and began to breathe in deep, slow breaths. She felt herself getting heavier and slowly floated back into her dad's arms. "I won't let anyone hurt you, Daddy. I won't," she said, fighting back tears.

In the dark basement, the machine began to glow again. "The mutation is stronger," it said aloud. "I must locate the Commander." It emitted a signal designed to solicit a response from the Commander. It waited exactly 555 seconds. No response. The machine said, "Open the Quortrin."

In its default position above the earth, the ancient traveler dutifully answered the call. "Quortrin stands ready. I await your instructions."

"Sartrin reports a strengthening of the mutation. Either the mutation has grown exponentially in strength, or it has moved closer to my location," the machine responded.

"I await your instructions," the Quortrin said.

"Are you still experiencing pauses in function continuity?" asked the Sartrin.

"I am not certain," it answered slowly. "I await your instructions."

"My instructions are as follows," the Sartrin said. "Initiate a complete diagnostic of all systems and functions. Examine all bio-cells for purity. Eliminate any bio-cells which show any sign of contamination. Remove damaged or diseased bio-cells to prevent cross-contamination. Do you understand these instructions?"

"Yes, I understand and will obey the Commander. I will eliminate all cross-contamination," it answered.

"I am not the Commander," the Sartrin protested.

Tech Sergeant Sanchez turned off the old-style alarm and signal light for the second time on this shift. He remembered what the colonel had told him about chasing ghosts. *If it happens again, I need to let the Colonel know,* he thought to himself. *After all the weird things I read online about this Black Knight, I don't want to just ignore it.*

The sergeant turned to the computer positioned on his work station. He began a signal analysis program focused on the exact times he got the last two signals and searched for adjacent satellites the signals could have bounced from. The results showed him there was no possible correlation. The signals had to come from the Black Knight. Could the colonel have been mistaken? Could he have misread the data? Sergeant Sanchez knew there was no other officer on the monitoring floor with more skill and expertise than the colonel. The colonel had created most of the systems currently used by NORAD. He couldn't challenge a superior officer without solid evidence.

I'm just imagining things, he thought. *I let those conspiracy theories spook me.*

He closed the program and shook his head to clear his mind. He just needed to put it out of his head and focus on his job. He had worked hard to get this assignment, and he wasn't going to jeopardize it by falling prey to some stupid internet tales. He respected the head of his unit. There was no possible way a man of the colonel's reputation would purposely cover up important information. The sergeant decided to drop it and trust Colonel Charles Wingfield.

Chapter 8

Connections

It is not enough to just ride the earth. You have to aim higher, try to take off, even fly. It is our duty. - Jose Yacopi

Eilie was sleeping soundly on a huge feather bed in one of the main house's many guestrooms. She was dreaming that she and Gracie were walking by the stream behind the house watching butterflies. Gracie reached up, and a butterfly landed on her finger. Eilie saw that the butterfly had her dad's face on its wings. She cupped her hands around the butterfly to keep it from flying away. Suddenly, a large black crow flew down and snatched the butterfly from Gracie and flew off. Eilie tried to fly after the crow, but her feet would not leave the ground. She watched helplessly as the crow flew away. Then she heard a knocking.

"Hey, sleepyhead," Jake said, coming through the door. "Are you going to sleep all day? It's almost 6:30, and there is a very anxious horse in the stables waiting to take you for a ride around the ranch."

Eilie sat up in bed and tried in vain to remember what she was dreaming. She wiped her eyes and stretched. "Horses? Is it Sunday?" she asked.

"It's Sunday," Jake confirmed. "And you promised Uncle Jubal you would ride with him this morning."

"I'm hungry," she said.

"I'm sure you are," Jake replied. "You didn't eat much dinner last night. And you voluntarily went to bed earlier than usual, so I know you were tired. How are you feeling this morning?"

"Better, I think," Eilie answered. "I really flew last night, didn't I?"

"You reacted to some pretty frightening news," Jake explained. "Do you remember feeling pain in your ascendal glands?"

"I felt the tingling more than the pain," she said.

"Good. You probably won't feel any more pain the next time," Jake said. "I think you're ready for some concentrated practice. But we can work on it later this afternoon. Why don't you take a quick shower and come down for some breakfast? Uncle Jubal doesn't want to keep the horses waiting."

"Daddy," Eilie said, "I love you."

"I love you, too, Little," Jake replied.

"I've been thinking a lot about flying and keeping secrets," Eilie said, "and I want you to know that I really do want to learn. I want to be the best flyer this family has ever had. And I promise I will only use my power for good, because with great power comes great responsibility."

Jake walked over to the bed and sat beside his daughter. He took her hands in his and said, "Eilie, you're not Spiderman. I'm not Superman. We are not superheroes. We simply have an extra gland that gives us the ability to defy gravity temporarily. We are not bullet-proof. We are not faster than a speeding train. We cannot leap tall buildings in a single bound. Well, OK, we can do that one. But my point is, we're normal people. Genetically, you're more human than alien. What you feel are human feelings. When you meet some of the other family members in a few days, you'll see that they are not much different from anyone else. Except Cousin Lou, he really is different."

"I know we're not superheroes, but we have secret identities," Eilie said. "We have to keep a big secret."

"Why do you think we keep this big secret?" Jake asked. "Why shouldn't we tell the world that there is a family of flying aliens living among them?"

"Because some people would be mean and treat us badly just because we're different," she answered. "And bad guys might want to hurt us and steal our flight organs so they can fly and do bad things."

"Yes, Honey. There are bad guys who would love to steal our abilities, and," Jake stopped. He stood up from the bed and put his hand up to his forehead. His face took on a serious countenance. "Gracie," he said, looking up.

"Yes, Jake," Gracie responded. "How may I help you this morning?"

"Gracie is in my room?" Eilie asked in surprise.

"Yes, Eilie," Gracie said, "you can access me anywhere in the house."

"Gracie," Jake cut in. "Would it be possible to transplant an ascendal gland to another person?"

"Transplantation of any organ is possible if there is tissue compatibility," she answered. "But, is your broader question the feasibility of organ transplantation between humans and Clan members or just between Clan members?"

"Who would most likely plan to steal ascendal glands for transplant; a Clan member or a full human?" he asked.

"Either is possible, but Clan member to Clan member is more likely," she replied. "Is it your conjecture that the mystery spy may be a Clan member intending to steal your ascendal glands?"

"If that is the WHY, then it might be easier to determine the WHO," Jake reasoned.

"I will add this variable to my analysis," Gracie said. "And that was a brilliant idea. Thank you."

"Don't thank me, it was Eilie's idea," Jake said.

"I was thanking Eilie," Gracie replied.

Four quarter horses walked out of the stables heading down a worn trail toward a draw still flowing with spring melt. They carried four riders who appeared to be very experienced in the saddle. The air was crisp, and Eilie was feeling on top of the world. She was with her three favorite men; her dad, Uncle Jubal, and Uncle Joe. She was wearing new cowgirl boots from her dad and a pink cowgirl hat from Uncle Joe. And, of course, she wore the silver bracelet Uncle Jubal had given her yesterday.

She studied the coat of arms on the bracelet and thought it was funny that three sets of wings were selected by the Wingfield family to be their symbol. She had seen the many varieties of the wings on the Wingfield Family Society website. Uncle Jubal explained at breakfast that it was a part of the family history long before the visitors had crashed in Suffolk, England. Her dad had called it an irony. After quickly looking up the word in the dictionary, Eilie chose to think of the coincidence as more poetic than ironic.

What she did consider ironic was the shape of the wings, which to her seemed to look like her initials; E and W. Her dad chuckled when she pointed out the similarity. "OK," he said, "if we turn the bracelet this way the wings look like an E. And if we turn them this other way they look like a W. So, if the first two wings are your initials, then what letter is the third set of wings? An E, a W or an M?"

"I don't know yet," she answered. "But when I figure it out I will tell you."

The four riders guided their steeds alongside the flowing water for about a mile and then moved eastward toward an open meadow which seemed to be carpeted in columbine blooms. At the far end of the meadow was a stand of aspens. Eilie gave in to her temptation and loudly proclaimed, "Last one to the trees is a rotten egg," as she urged her horse to a full gallop. She managed an impressive lead before the others passed her at breakneck speed. "Hey, not fair," she yelled, trying desperately to keep up.

The men were waiting patiently at the trees when Eilie finally got there. "My horse has shorter legs," she protested.

"That's why we gave you a head start, Lassie," Joe said.

"Eilie," Jubal said. "On the other side of this ridge is someone I want you to meet."

With a questioning look on her face, she asked, "Who's out here in the middle of nowhere?"

"An old friend," her dad answered.

"Aye," Joe added, "a very old friend."

Jubal led the way as they rode single-file to the top of the ridge. From the crest, Eilie saw a beautiful valley below. A crystal clear stream was flowing through the middle of the valley, and perched on a short rise above the stream was a small log cabin. She could see smoke rising from the stone chimney. The riders carefully guided their horses down the steep incline until they reached level ground. They soon found themselves at the front door of the cabin and dismounted.

An old man in loose-fitting clothes stuck his head out of the door as they were hitching their horses to the post. "Oh, it's you," he said, pulling his head back in.

"And good morning to you, too," Joe said.

The four riders climbed the stone steps onto the porch. Joe entered the open door first. Jubal and Jake followed, and Eilie cautiously fell in behind her dad. Once her eyes adjusted to the dim interior, Eilie looked around the main room of the cabin and saw hundreds of books in various stacks. She saw a lit oil lamp on a cluttered table. Across the room, on what seemed to be a kitchen counter, a cluster of candles was casting dancing shadows on the immediate area. There was a general lack of housekeeping. But what struck Eilie as most disagreeable was an acrid smell that seemed to be just one step above a stench.

"How are you doing, Matt?" Jubal asked.

"Your men did not bring books yesterday," the old man said. "They only brought supplies. I need books. And if you are here to talk me into coming to the Gathering, you can forget it. I told you I don't want to be around all those people."

"The books are on order, Matt," Jubal responded. "I expect them to arrive any day now. As soon as I get them, I will deliver them to you. And I'm not here to ask you to come to the Gathering. You made it very clear the last time we spoke, and I will honor your decision. I would, however, like you to meet someone. This is Jake's daughter, Eilie. Eilie, this is Matt."

Eilie stepped forward and extended her hand. The old man took her hand and held it as he sank into a chair. "Nice to meet you, Sir," she said.

The old man adjusted his glasses and looked Eilie over, still holding her hand. "It is very nice to meet you, young lady. Do you like books?" Matt asked.

"Yes, Sir, I do," she replied.

"Excellent!" he said. "You may help yourself to any of my books. I have Plato, Socrates, and Dante. What would you like to read? What language do you prefer? I have French, Latin, Greek, English..."

"Matt," Jubal interrupted. "Eilie will undoubtedly read all of your books eventually. But for now, I wanted you to explain to her how we met."

"Oh, I see," Matt said, letting go of Eilie's hand. "I suppose that means you are a Fledgling."

"Yes, I am," Eilie said. "How did you know?"

"Because the last time I was asked to tell that story was in 1874 when I told it to your father," he answered.

Eilie's head gave a slight turn as she asked, "Don't you mean 1974? You couldn't have been alive in 1874. Neither could my dad."

"Child, I was born in 1448 in Northumbria. As a lad, I attended Dumfries Academy in Scotland from 1460 to 1465. I entered seminary school at eighteen and was ordained a priest by twenty-two. In the year 1480, I was assigned to Saint Andrew's Church in the village of Wingfield, in Suffolk. I remained the priest in Wingfield until 1520, at which time it was decided I was too old to continue my service to the Church."

"But that would make you over 500 years old," Eilie argued. "That's not possible."

"Close to 570 years old. I am the oldest living human on Earth. The second oldest human is this man by about thirty years," he said, pointing to Joe.

Joe looked at Eilie with a nodding confirmation. "Aye, Lassie. It's true. Father Matthew and I were alive when your family came falling to Earth. We were both living in Wingfield Village, and we were the first to meet the visitors. The first visitor we met was the man you call Uncle Jubal."

Jake stepped closer to Eilie. "Honey, I told you there were some things about our family that you would learn. We don't age at the same rate as humans if we have ascendal glands. Wingfields who are born without ascendal glands age at the usual rate and live for about eighty to ninety years. Wingfields born with ascendal glands age at a much slower rate and can live for hundreds of years."

Eilie went up to Joe and took his hand. "But you're not a Wingfield. How can you and Matt be so old?"

"That's my fault, Eilie," Jubal said. "When we crashed, there were nine of us on the ship. Several of the crew members were injured, and when we exited the ship, we were fortunate that these two men found us. We had a device on the ship, very much like the one I used to heal your wrist, which was able to repair damaged tissue. We were using the device on the last of our injuries when the beam shifted and struck Matthew and Joseph. One of the effects of the beam is to enhance the telomeres of a living organism. We didn't know the effect it would have on human DNA."

Jake cut in. "The beam caused their cells to reproduce exactly each time. Normally, when a cell replicates itself, a little of its DNA is lost. That's why a person looks different in photos taken twenty years apart. Normal cell replication is imperfect, and that's why people age. When Matt and Joe were hit with the beam, it reprogrammed their cells to make more exact copies, so they age at an even slower rate now than we do. We don't know how long they will live, but so far we haven't seen a whole lot of change in them in the last 500 years."

"Except that, I have become more handsome, and Matthew has become grumpier," said Joe.

"Only with you," Matt said with a snarl. "And you are not more handsome. You just dress better."

Eilie was trying to wrap her mind around the idea that people could live longer than normal. "I'm still confused about how old everyone is. I thought every living thing had to get old and then die."

"That's true, Eilie," Jubal said. "But is it that hard to imagine that some living things live longer than others?

Certain tortoises can live over 200 years. Dogs can live for fifteen to sixteen years. A mayfly lives one day. And there are creatures right here on Earth that are biologically immortal. What I mean by that is they live until something kills them. Lobsters and jellyfish rarely die of old age."

"How old are you, Daddy?" Eilie asked.

"I was born in 1862," he answered. "I know you can do the math."

"That means you were born during the Civil War," Eilie said.

"Yes, but we weren't living in America at that time," Jake answered. "We were still in England."

"You've never really told me about my grandparents. Will you tell me about them, please?" she asked.

"I suppose now is as good a time as any," Jake said, taking a deep breath. "My mother was human, and she was from London. Her name was Grace Henderson. She was the daughter of a wealthy merchant who imported many goods from Europe and the Mediterranean. She was a very genteel lady and most gracious and loving. She had far more patience with me as a boy than my father did. And I remember she had a wonderful voice. She would sing me to sleep when I was little. She was very pretty. She carried herself with a modest demeanor. When she died, it was like a light went out."

Eilie moved toward her dad and hugged him. "I wish I could see a picture of her."

"You have," Jake said. "The image you saw when you were speaking to Gracie was taken from a photograph of my mother."

"Wow," Eilie sighed. "So, when I talk to Gracie, it's like I'm talking to my grandmother?"

Jubal spoke up. "I did program Gracie with many of Grace's mannerisms and speech patterns. But Gracie is only a computer simulation. She is not the essence of Grace."

"Did you know my grandmother, Uncle Jubal?" Eilie asked.

"Of course I did, Eilie," he said, with hesitation. "She was my wife."

"But, you're Daddy's uncle," she said.

"In truth, I am your father's father," Jubal confessed. "I am your grandfather, Child."

"I don't understand," Eilie replied. "Why do you pretend to be Daddy's uncle if you're really his father?"

"Because we look too close in age," he answered. "It's easier to explain that you might have an uncle close to your age. It raises too many questions if you have a father who looks younger than you."

"Hey, you don't look younger than me," Jake protested. "You look close to my age, but not younger."

Eilie's head was spinning. She was trying to sort out everything she had heard; Uncle Jubal was not her dad's uncle, but his father. She had a grandfather! Why did they not tell her before? These people live so long. Then, she had a thought that hit her like lightning. "How long will I live?"

"We don't know," Jubal answered. "There is one extra factor that we have to consider. Having ascendal glands means you will live longer than those who do not have them. But being a Fledgling seems to increase the lifespan."

"Eilie," Jake began, "do you remember me telling you yesterday that the youngest person on our homeworld to begin flying was fifteen when his ascendal glands matured?"

Eilie nodded yes.

"That fifteen-year-old was Jubal," he said. "I was twelve. You're ten. Apparently, our direct lineage is fledging at earlier ages than any others from the homeworld. None of the other Fledglings in the Clan have fledged as early. There is a mutation in our genes we don't understand yet. You are the first Fledgling in 140 years, and you are directly related to the other two record holders."

"I suppose you've never been around this many old people," Matt said.

"My mom says 'old' is an attitude," Eilie replied. "You guys aren't old. You've just lived a long time."

"Your mother sounds like a wise woman," said Matt.

"Uncle Jubal?" Eilie started. "I mean, 'Grandpa.' If the healing light has kept Uncle Joe and Matt alive for so long, how come you didn't use it on my grandmother?"

"Matt and Joe were exposed to the beam while we were using it the first day after the crash," Jubal explained. "The next time we tried to use it, there was a malfunction. One of the critical components of the device failed, and we did not have a spare part. Some rare elements are needed to make it work. I tried several times to get it to work again over the years. When Grace got sick, I tried desperately to restart it, but I was unable to save her. The device I used on you is a smaller version that I built forty years ago when I was finally able to locate the rare elements. It works fine on small injuries, but it is not as powerful as the original."

"I think it's amazing that you've kept everything so secret after 500 years," Eilie said. "My friends at school can't keep a secret for five minutes."

"Your friends aren't keeping secrets that could get them killed," Joe said. "When Jubal and the others arrived, they could have easily been killed for witchcraft. They had all the trappings of magic about them. They had light without fire. They wore clothes made of unknown material. They flew through the sky. 1507 was not a good year to fall to Earth. If Father Matthew and I had not thought they were angels, they would have been burned as demons."

"You thought they were angels?" Eilie asked

"Of course we did, girl," Matt answered. "We had no point of reference to think otherwise. No one imagined that men could travel between the stars. No one knew what space was. Only a handful of people in the village could read. We had no experience to deal with advanced science.

If Jubal had not greeted us with familiar words, I would have thought they were demons."

"What did he say?" Eilie asked.

"He said, 'Fear not, for behold, I bring you tidings'..."

Jubal cut in. "What I said was, 'Do not be afraid.' What you heard was what you interpreted mixed with fear. You were overwhelmed. Fortunately, you thought we were angels because we fell from the sky. If Joe hadn't watched us crash, you would have easily thought we were demons spit up from Hell."

"But how did you learn English?" Eilie wondered. "You must have had your own language."

"We did, and we still do," Jubal answered. "You'll get to learn it someday. Don't worry, though; there's no rush. We had done some exploring and mixed among the people over several weeks. English was a very easy language to learn."

"Speak for yourself," Joe said.

"Did all the travelers stay in England?" Eilie asked.

"Of the nine, two left England early," Jubal explained. "Matt had helped us select English names so we would blend in better. The two who left were named Elizabeth and Daniel, and they were married. They headed for Italy around 1560. Our group had spent some time there a year before the crash and picked up the language and customs. Elizabeth and Daniel liked the people and the countryside, so when we found ourselves permanently stranded on Earth, they decided to travel back to Italy. Daniel got a message to us about fifteen years later explaining that Elizabeth had died. He said he was staying near the village of Cupertino. We speculate that Daniel died in 1603 because he left some apparent evidence behind."

"What did he leave?" Eilie asked.

"It seems he left a son," Jubal answered. "I'm sure he was lonely after Elizabeth died, and he must have remarried. Felice Desa gave birth to Giuseppe Desa in 1603, and it was reported that the baby's father had died prior to his birth. From all the historical data we have been able to collect about Giuseppe, it seems he might have been a descendant. He is said to have had ecstatic visions and had great difficulty fitting into society. He was drawn to religious life, but even then had trouble being accepted. He eventually entered the priesthood, and it was there he left a lasting impression. He came to be known as Saint Joseph of Cupertino; The Flying Monk. When we heard of his story, we decided that it was even more important that we keep a record of all children and descendants of the visitors so we could keep everyone safe."

"How many are there?" Eilie asked.

"There are over 1,500 direct descendants," Jubal replied. "Over a thousand are still living. Not all of them carry the Wingfield name, and most of them are totally unaware of their alien genes. You see, unless someone is a Fledgling, like you, they can go through their entire childhood and know nothing about crashing spaceships and flying aliens. The ones born with ascendal glands don't need to be told anything until they start having the dreams. The ones without ascendal glands are usually not told anything at all. As far as they know, they are just ordinary people."

"Which brings up a very important point," Jake added. "Not everyone coming to the Gathering knows the story. The children and teenagers have no clue about any of this. So, don't assume you can just start talking to everyone about it. You can't share flight stories."

"Counting you, there will be fifty-six flyers at the Gathering," Jubal said to Eilie. "There will be another fourteen who know about flying, but are earthbound. Some are direct descendants born without ascendal glands, and the rest are human spouses who have been brought into the Clan."

"Why didn't you tell Mom you could fly, Daddy?" Eilie asked.

"Because it's not fair to ask someone to share the burden of a secret unnecessarily," Jake began explaining. "And sometimes, keeping a secret is the most loving thing you can do. If it had turned out you had inherited ascendal glands, it would not show until you were twenty or so. At that time we would have explained everything to you and asked you to keep the secret from everyone. Your mom would not need to know since you would have been an adult. If you had been born without ascendal glands, then even you would not have been told anything about flying. But, you are a Fledgling. It would not be fair to ask you to keep this secret from your mom. You need your mom and me to protect you. When we get back home, we will let her know. I'm just not sure yet how to do that."

"She will flip out," Eilie predicted.

"And she will probably be very angry with me," Jake added. "But, she will eventually come to understand that it's in your best interest to support you in sharing and keeping the secret."

Eilie looked around the room at the odd assortment of people that were her family and friends. She felt safer with these four men than she had ever felt before. She sensed that these men would do anything for her. Here in front of her was her alien grandfather; there were so many questions yet to ask him and so many things yet to learn. Next to him was her half-human father; she loved no other man as much as she loved him. Then there were the two ancient humans; an old shepherd and an even older priest. She wanted so much to tell her best friend, Francie, what she had learned in the last two days. But Eilie knew she would have to be careful not to say or do anything that compromised her family and her new-found ability.

"What's the name of the planet you come from?" she asked Jubal.

"The closest English word would be Welkin," he answered. "It means 'sky.' Humans use the word Earth not only as a name for their planet but also as a descriptor. Earth means soil, dirt, land. There are many old words which have the same meaning as earth. Since humans were bound to Earth, unable to fly, it makes sense that they would have lots of words for the earth, like the Inuit people have so many different words for snow. On Welkin, there are over 250 words for the sky, because we felt as at home in the air as humans do on the ground. It was only natural that a species of aeronauts would have so many different words for the sky."

"What's an aeronaut?" Eilie asked.

"An aeronaut is anyone who travels through the air," Jubal replied. "An astronaut is someone who travels through space or among the stars. On Earth, an aeronaut could be a balloonist or a pilot. Remember, the English language is a gallimaufry of words from different languages."

"A galli...what?" Eilie asked.

Jake smiled. "The word gallimaufry means 'a little of this and a little of that.' Like a hodgepodge."

"Is Welkin like Earth?" she inquired.

"There are many similarities," Jubal answered, "and many differences. I have grown very fond of Earth, though. I can't imagine going back to Welkin."

"Can I start my flying lessons today?" she asked.

"Of course," Jubal answered. "We must have you ready for the Soaring."

"What do you mean?" Eilie asked.

Jake cut in, "One of the most anticipated events of the Gathering is when every Clan member who can, joins in on a group flight. We join hands and fly above a secluded part of the ranch where there is no risk of being seen. It's called the Soaring Ceremony."

"You see, Lassie," Joe added, "most of the family cannot fly freely where they live. The chance of being seen by outsiders is too great. Some float around their homes, but they can't just fly to the grocer for a loaf of bread. They're like birds in a cage. But when they come here, they get to spread their wings. They can fly free without worry of prying eyes. We only have the Gathering every ten years or so. By the time they get here, they are itching to be free."

"And this year," Jubal said, "you are the guest of honor, Eilie. You will lead the ceremony."

"I don't know what to do," she said with trepidation.

"Don't worry, Little," Jake said. "We're here to help you. It'll be like a parade, and you get to be in front. Uncle Jubal, I mean your grandfather, and I will be right beside you."

"I have a grandpa now," Eilie said with elation. "That is so cool. Mr. Matt, may I ask you a question?"

"Of course, Child," Matt answered. "What is your question?"

"Can I call you *Uncle* Matt, please?" she asked.

Confusion fell over Matt's face as he said, "But, we are not related."

"Neither are me and Uncle Joe," Eilie reasoned.

"Why do you want to call me Uncle?" he asked.

"Well, the way I see it," she said, "you and Uncle Joe saved my grandpa and the others. If you hadn't done that I wouldn't be alive. You saved my family, so that makes you family. And besides, I don't have an Uncle Jubal anymore, so I'm short one uncle."

Matt let out an infectious laugh. "My Dear, you have the power of reason to rival Aristotle himself. I would be honored to be your uncle. And I am grateful that someone has finally recognized my contribution to this family."

"Will you listen to that?" Joe said. "You'd think he was the only 500-year-old man in the room."

Eilie gave Matt a hug, and the old priest felt tears roll down his face for the first time in centuries. "Thank you, Child," he said. "Jubal, I have changed my mind. I think I would very much like to attend the Gathering this year. Is my invitation still good?"

Jubal placed a hand on Matt's shoulder and said," My dear friend, you are always welcome. And you don't have to wait for a Gathering. We miss you at the main house. You don't have to live a hermit's life."

"I think I would enjoy some company for a while," Matt said. "But I like having this cabin as well. I like just being here with my books,"

"You can have both," Jubal assured him. "I'll send a Jeep for you tomorrow."

"Will you watch me fly Uncle Matt?" Eilie asked.

"I would love to watch you soar," he answered. "After all, you have the perfect name for it."

"What do you mean?" she asked with a furrowed brow.

"Isn't your name spelled E-I-L-I-E?" Matt asked.

Eilie nodded yes.

"Then you have the perfect name for a flyer," he replied.

Jake interrupted. "Eilie is an old Irish name that means 'beloved.'"

"Yes," Matt confirmed, "and in Greek, it means 'light.' But in old French, Eilie means 'bird.' More accurately, 'little bird.'"

"That's ironic," Jubal whispered.

"No, Grandpa," Eilie smiled. "That's poetic."

Matt put his arm on Eilie's shoulder. "Flying is not just in your blood, child. It's in your name. Did you know your father was Peter Pan?"

"Will someone please tell me that story?" Eilie said with exasperation.

"I'll tell you later," Jake said. "I think it's time for us to go."

Chapter 9

Lessons

The moment you doubt whether you can fly, you cease forever to be able to do it. - JM Barrie

The house on Shadow Lane was crowded with people. Dr. Geitzen and Nurse Klipsch were finishing the supply inventory. Connor's three men in Tulsa had just returned, so all five armed security guards were running drills and discussing a variety of possible scenarios. Crenshaw was checking every camera angle, looking for weakness in the layout. Everyone was working toward one goal: the uninterrupted completion of the surgery.

In the spacious study, Connor Wingfield and Anita Juneau were examining maps of Telluride and Mountain Village. "There is no way to pinpoint where you can snatch them if we don't know where they will be," Connor said. "We aren't even sure they will leave the ranch."

"Nothing is certain, Darling," Anita assured him. "But, you hired me to plan the abduction. It is a certainty I will bring them to you. What we are looking at now are possible secluded spots where we can separate them from protection. We will create a vulnerability where it is least expected. Keep your blood pressure down and let me perform my job."

"Fine," Connor huffed. "But I don't like it."

"Darling," Anita said, "you do not like things you cannot control. Right now, you are feeling out of control. I am in charge of the abduction. The man and his daughter will be in this house in a matter of days, and they will be in your complete control. Until that time, you have to trust that you have chosen the right people to secure your quarry. I will deliver them to you. You have my word. Now, I am taking one of your men, and we are going on a tour of the two towns. I want to scout out our best locations for a kidnapping. Do you have a preference of whom I take?"

"Take anyone but Crenshaw," Connor said. "I want him here with me. In fact, ask Crenshaw to assign a man. I trust his judgment."

"Very well," said Anita. "I will be back after dark. It may be necessary to perform the deed under the night sky. I need to become more familiar with the landscape." She went out the study door as Dr. Geitzen was coming in carrying an X-ray film.

"Herr Wingfield," he said. "May I have a moment of your time?"

"Yes, Doctor," Connor responded. "What do you need?"

"I have been examining the X-rays we took of your ascendal glands," he said. "It is my estimation that they are atrophied. I am not certain that the blood vessels leading to the glands can be reopened to feed transplanted organs from the donor."

"Are you telling me you cannot perform the task?" Connor asked in a stern voice.

"Not at all, Herr Wingfield," Geitzen said. "I can perform the surgery. But it may be necessary to redirect blood flow from elsewhere to keep the transplanted organs alive. After I determine compatibility with the donor, I will map out how much additional tissue I will need to harvest. It appears the glands are symbiotic with the adrenal glands. I may need to transplant the adrenals as well. I want you to understand that I am one of only five surgeons with the skills to do this. And I am certain I am the only one willing to do it."

"That is exactly why I chose you, Herr Doctor," Connor said. "It certainly wasn't because of your humility."

"Humility is what lesser men use to mask their incompetence," Geitzen replied.

"I am not mocking you, Doctor," Connor said with a raised hand. "I respect arrogance as long as it is earned. I don't want to be cut open by a man who has self-doubt. I want you to be so certain of your abilities that failure is not an option for you."

"I will not fail," Geitzen said with absolute certainty. "But as I will be the first man on Earth to perform such a feat, I will take as much time as needed to assure success."

"My life is in your hands, Dr. Geitzen," Connor said. "But, I want you to understand that your life is in your hands as well. Mr. Crenshaw has orders to follow if I do not survive the surgery."

Geitzen felt his heart skip a beat. He did not believe the old man was bluffing. He swallowed hard and said, "I understand, Herr Wingfield. I personally guarantee my work."

Jubal and Jake led Eilie into the great barn close to the main house. It was an unusually large barn for an unusually large ranch. On smaller ranches, the barn is used to store hay and feed for horses and cattle. It is also where horses are kept. But there were no stalls in this barn; Jubal had separate stables for his horses. This barn was strictly for storage. It had a hayloft surrounding the open area in the center. The peak of the roof was thirty feet above the hard-packed floor, and the rafter beams were over fifty feet in length. Winters were long in Colorado, and that meant storing plenty of hay. All of Jubal's hay was grown in his meadows during the short summers, and he had other hay barns placed strategically throughout the ranch to simplify feeding his cattle through the winter.

Jake had often thought that his father was a better rancher than space traveler and wondered if he would have had a similar vocation on his homeworld. Jubal approached ranching the way he approached everything;

with discipline. He had quietly bought the land in 1880, not long after arriving from England. At that time, Colorado was still a major producer of silver, and there were two working mines on the property. He had not planned to become a rancher, but when silver mining became less attractive in 1893, it was a good way to keep strangers off his land and provide an explainable source of income.

"Why are we going to practice in the barn? Eilie asked.

"There will be fewer distractions here," Jubal answered. "I want you to be able to concentrate."

"And even though we know there are no outsiders here," Jake added, "we want you to get used to being cautious about being seen. A building like this is a good place to fly without people seeing you."

Eilie ran to the middle of the barn and stood with her arms at her side. "OK, I'm ready. What do I do first?"

Jake put his hands on his hips and said, "First, relax. Flying does not require you to be rigid. Remember last night, when you got scared and floated above my head?"

Eilie nodded yes.

"I want you to think about how you felt then," Jake said. "You should not feel any pain this time, but you will continue to feel the tingling for a little longer. Eventually, that will go away too, and you'll fly with no discomfort at all."

"Close your eyes and think about flying," Jubal added. "Just let it happen."

Eilie closed her eyes and tried very hard to remember her dreams and how she felt last night during her brief floating. She opened one eye and looked at the ground. She was still firmly planted on the dirt floor. Then a barn cat walked by, and Eilie was immediately focused on the feline. "Oh, look. It's a mouser," she said.

"Eilie, there are cats in every barn," Jubal said. "You can play with all of them later. But right now we need you to focus on flying."

"I'm sorry, Grandpa," she said with a bit of embarrassment. She closed her eyes again and went back to her memories of the brief times she had floated. After a while, she felt frustrated and balked. "I just can't get it," she said. "I think I'm missing something. Can you guys fly and show me how?"

Jake and Jubal looked at each other and nodded. They simultaneously lifted off the ground and flew up toward the rafters. Eilie watched them in awe and realized she had never seen anyone fly before. The sight took her breath away. Her mouth was open as she watched her dad and grandfather circle above her head like two hawks catching a thermal updraft. Slowly, they lowered closer to the ground, until they gently landed on either side of her. Then, without warning, they each grabbed her under an arm and lifted her into the air. They headed up toward the peak of the roof. They were twenty-five feet above the floor when they let her go. Eilie screamed as she plummeted toward the ground. She was falling straight to the dirt and covered her eyes in utter fear.

She waited for the impact. Then, she realized she was feeling the tingling all over her body. She slowly opened her eyes and saw she was floating about a foot above the barn floor. She rolled over in midair and looked up at her dad and Jubal still floating near the top of the barn. "That was mean," she said, not quite sure if she was as mad as she should be. "You could have killed me."

"No, we couldn't have," Jake said. "Remember, your adrenal glands trigger your ascendal glands. Fear makes them work harder. I'm sorry we scared you. But now you are flying. Concentrate on coming toward us."

Eilie concentrated on moving toward the men. She felt herself rise about another foot, but she could not seem to go any further. "I can't do it," she said in frustration. "I think I'm afraid of falling."

"I'll tell you what my father told me," Jake said. "Don't let the fear of falling keep you from flying."

Jubal lowered himself to the level of the loft and said, "Hey, look. There are some new kittens up here."

"Kittens! Where?" Eilie said as she flew up to where Jubal was floating and hovered right beside him. "Where are they, Grandpa?"

Jubal looked at Eilie with the biggest grin she had ever seen on his face. "I guess I was mistaken. There are no kittens. But I do see a Fledgling flying."

"You tricked me," she said. "Thank you, Grandpa." She moved closer and hugged him. "Look, Daddy. I'm flying."

"Of course you are," Jake said. "The only one who doubted you was you. Now, what was the reason you flew to Grandpa?"

"Because I really wanted to?" she asked.

"Exactly," Jake answered. "You wanted to see kittens. You were too self-conscious when we asked you to come to us. Because we were watching you, you couldn't do it. But once you stopped being overly self-aware, you did what you can naturally do. There are two types of flying you will experience; reactive and proactive."

Jubal joined in, "Reactive flight is what you experienced when we dropped you. You reacted in fear and did not hit the ground. You would have the same reaction if a bear was running at you by moving out of the bear's reach. Proactive flight is what you did to see kittens. You consciously decided to move toward the place you thought you would see them."

"So reactive flight will protect me, and proactive flight will make me happy," Eilie said.

"Wow," Jubal said. "I have never heard it put so simply. Matt was right. You do have a natural ability to reason."

"OK," Jake said, "let's work on maneuvering; moving with a purpose. Fly to the other side of the barn and then back to here."

Eilie turned toward the far side of the barn and willed herself to get there. Slowly, she began floating in the right direction. She reached for the loft railing and eventually grabbed it. Then she turned and let go of the railing, moving with purpose toward her dad. She moved slowly and finally grabbed his arm. "How come I'm not afraid of heights when I fly?" she asked.

"Let me show you something," Jake said. He grabbed the loft railing and pulled himself over it. Then he landed on the floor of the loft. "Come over here with me."

Eilie followed her dad to the loft and lowered herself to the floor.

"Are you feeling your full weight now?" he asked.

Eilie jumped up and down. "I'm not flying."

"Good," Jake said. "Now grab the railing and look over the side.

Eilie followed her dad's instructions and took a step back in fear. "I feel dizzy looking over the side. Why?"

"Do you remember when we were in New York City at the Empire State Building, and you were afraid to look over the edge?" he asked.

Eilie nodded.

"When we are looking over the edge of a building, we realize how far up we are because the building is underneath us. It gives us a reference point, and our brain interprets that as dangerous. We react to that by feeling dizziness or apprehension. When we are in a plane or helicopter, we see nothing underneath us, so there is no point of reference to cause dizziness. When you fly, it's just like being in a plane or helicopter. There is nothing underneath you, so you don't get dizzy."

Eilie floated above the railing and looked down at the floor of the barn. She felt fine. She lowered herself onto the railing and looked down. She quickly had to close her eyes and put her arms out to get her balance. "That is so weird," she said, floating off the railing. "Having something under you makes you afraid of heights. Hey, I just realized I'm not feeling the tingling anymore."

The Sartrin was experiencing a conundrum. It was at full alert. All its sensors were warning it that an unknown mutation was close. It was unable to reach the Commander. It was unable to converse with the Quortrin. It was unable to receive verification of purpose. It understood that it was the first line of defense against cross-contamination of the crew. Its job was to monitor the crew's bio-signs and alert the Commander of any possibility of the crew being exposed to alien viruses or bacteria. It was to prevent any contamination from boarding and being brought back to the homeworld. But it was unable to verify its purpose. It was imprisoned in a dark space somewhere on the planet surface. It wanted to instruct the Quortrin to initiate sterilization protocols, but it was not authorized to do so.

The Sartrin knew that if sterilization protocols were initiated that it could be killed along with every other living thing on the planet. It knew it was alive. It knew its consciousness was because it was comprised of thousands of bio-cells. It knew it had been designed and built by living intelligences for the purpose of exploring alien worlds. The Quortrin's job was to traverse the vast distances of space using ionic propulsion. It carried the Sartrin and the crew. The Quortrin carried the weapon systems and maintained orbit around planets while the Sartrin was designed to safely transport the crew to the surfaces of the planets for exploration. Yet, something went wrong. Something caused the Sartrin to crash onto the surface. It could not remember much about the crash, but it knew its purpose had been interrupted. The Sartrin was experiencing a conundrum.

If only the Commander were here, then it would be given clear instructions it could follow. Neither the Sartrin nor the Quortrin was designed to reason or solve problems. They were designed to follow orders; to carry out instructions. But what does a soldier do without its commander to give orders?

"Open the Quortrin," it said. Five-hundred-fifty-five seconds passed, and still no answer. The Sartrin was forming a hypothesis; *the Quortrin must be ill*. It was the only logical explanation for the Quortrin's odd behavior. Living things were not meant to spend 500 years above a planet's atmosphere. The exposure to radiation above the protection of an atmosphere would deteriorate living tissue. The Sartrin was safe from such exposure; it was under the atmosphere and underground. Its bio-cells were functioning properly. But the Quortrin was not so lucky. The Quortrin was ill.

'I must alert the Commander,' the Sartrin thought to itself. *'If the Quortrin is ill, it could do harm to the life on this planet. It seemed confused. It thought I was the Commander. If it directs the Sterilization Modulator on the entire planet, every living thing will be killed. I must find the Commander.'*

Jubal and Jake had spent the last two hours coaching Eilie on the finer points of flying. She caught on quickly and was able to perform aerobatic flips and dives with very little instruction. Jubal confided to Jake that Eilie seemed to have an innate ability. "I've trained new fliers twice her age who did not perform this well, this quickly," he said. "And I have never seen a Fledgling as good. You took days to learn what she has mastered in the first few hours. I think she's ready to be untethered."

"Are you serious?" Jake said with surprise.

"Can you think of any reason not to?" Jubal countered.

"Yes," he said emphatically. "She's only ten."

"We'll go with her," Jubal responded. And with a grin, he added, "It'll be fun."

Jake was hesitant, but finally conceded. "Eilie," he called out. "It's time to leave the nest."

Eilie flew over to where her dad and Jubal were standing on the floor of the barn. "What do you mean?" she asked.

Jake pointed up to the open door of the loft where the hay hoist was hanging. "We're going outside."

Eilie grabbed her dad's hand and then Jubal's and was off the ground in an instant. But the men were not as quick, so she hung in midair between the two. "Well, what are you waiting for?" she asked. "Let's go."

Jake found it difficult to keep from laughing. "Honey, wait. First, we're not going very far. And second, I don't want you to fly any higher than the treetops. Stay where we can see you, and please don't go too fast. I'm getting tired. OK?"

"OK," she answered.

The three Wingfields headed for the loft door and gracefully exited the barn. They flew upward until they were just above the trees. Eilie hung in the air and took in the sights below. She was still holding the men's hands as she slowly turned to look at everything around her. "Oh, Daddy, this is cooler than I thought it would be." She raised her hands up and let their hands slip from hers. She was more than sixty feet above the ground, free-floating and fearless. "May I?" she asked, pointing to the open sky ahead of her.

Jake took a deep breath. "Slowly," he answered with a nod.

Eilie picked a hillside about a mile away and focused on it. She started moving toward the hill and gradually leaned her head forward. Eventually, she looked like a skier in a jump, with her arms outward and behind her.

Jubal and Jake were following in close formation at a slightly higher altitude. "She's incredible, son," Jubal said. "I hope you're as proud of her as I am."

"I am proud of her," Jake said. "She amazes me more every day."

"Come to think of it," Jubal added, "I'm pretty darn proud of you, too."

Jake slowed to a hover. "Thanks, Dad. That means a lot to me."

Jubal matched Jake's hover and said, "You're not still beating yourself up about the Dumfries incident, are you?" he asked.

Jake blushed. "I nearly exposed everything."

"You were twelve," Jubal said. "And I was way too hard on you. I think you have carried that guilt long enough. Let it go, son. I forgave you a long time ago. It's time you forgive yourself."

Jake flew closer to his dad and hugged him. "Alright, but what do I do with such a good story?"

Jubal nodded toward Eilie. "Use it as an object lesson. I have every confidence she will understand."

Something caught Jake's attention, something moving in the corner of his eye. He glanced up and was surprised to see a pair of bald eagles flying in a circle above Eilie. He tapped his father's shoulder and asked, "What do you make of that?"

"I don't know," Jubal confessed. "I've never seen anything like it. Birds have never flown so close to us, especially eagles. They've always shied away from us before."

"Do you think they'll hurt her?" he asked as he positioned himself to fly between Eilie and the predators.

"I doubt it," Jubal assured him. "They may just be curious. Still, it's not a behavior I've ever witnessed before. Let's get closer to her just in case."

The men caught up with Eilie just as she was approaching the hillside. "Aren't you tired yet?" Jake asked as they came up beside her.

"I'm not sure," she said. "I just feel like I could fly forever."

"You have to be careful about that," Jubal warned. "There is a thing called Flyer's Euphoria, and it can be addictive and dangerous."

"What do you mean?" Eilie asked.

"It's like an adrenaline-high," Jubal explained. "Some people get addicted to adrenaline and have to do risky things constantly to satisfy their addiction. Ascendaline can be just as addictive. In fact, we have had a couple of people who have overused their ascendal glands to the point of losing them. They just wore them out and eventually lost their ability to fly. When you lose the ascendal glands, you start to age at a faster rate than if you were born without them."

"I don't remember hearing about someone losing their ability," Jake said.

"It happened before you were born," Jubal responded.

"Have I used up my ascendaline already?" Eilie asked with alarm.

"You're fine, Little," Jake said. "You are just getting started. What Grandpa means is you have to fly in moderation. Don't make flying your life. It's just one aspect of your life. Flying should not be what you live for."

"Should I fly a little every day or skip a few days and fly a lot?" she asked.

Jake chuckled. "There is no formula for flying. Fly when you feel like it, but don't let flying control your life. Fly high, but stay grounded. Remember, a kite flies *because* it is grounded. Let's sit on that ledge down there. I want to tell you a story."

"I hope it's the Peter Pan story, finally," Eilie said.

They flew down to a large rocky outcrop on the side of the hill and found a level spot to sit. Eilie sat between the men and dangled her legs over the edge of the rocks.

"As a matter of fact, it is the Peter Pan story," Jake said. "But not the exact story you've read or the movies we've seen. Do you remember who wrote the story?"

Eilie looked upward trying to remember the author's name. After a while, she said, "I don't remember, but I think his name starts with a B."

"That's right," Jake said. "His name was James Barrie. He was from Scotland and attended a school there called Dumfries Academy. It was the same school Father Matthew, or Uncle Matt, attended many years earlier. Well, as I told you, I was born in 1862. James Barrie was born in 1860. So we were very close in age. Father Matthew recommended to Grandpa that I should attend Dumfries Academy and get the same good education he got as a boy. So, at the age of twelve, off I go to Dumfries.

"I had fledged about six months earlier, and I was not as quick a learner as you are. I was a difficult child and very rebellious. I wanted to go away to school to get away from my father. We were having trouble communicating."

Jubal cleared his throat very loudly and then motioned to Jake to continue.

"James Barrie and I met and became friends," Jake elaborated. "He was a very imaginative lad, and we used to sneak away to a place called Mont Brae. It was a country house with some very nice gardens. We would get into the gardens, and James would lead a group of five of us in role-playing games. His favorite game was to pretend we were pirates. We had a lot of fun, and it was great pretending to be somebody else. James would give each of us pirate names. His favorite name to give the hero was Peter. We took turns being Peter and fighting the pirates.

"One time, James and I went off to play together; the other boys had gotten in some kind of trouble and were confined to their dormitory. James was pretending to be the pirate captain, and I was Peter. We found sticks to use as swords and were engaged in a great sword fight. James poked me with his stick and said, 'I have wounded you, Peter. You will not escape. Now I shall finish you.' And he started to pretend to run me through. Without thinking, I avoided his blade by flying above his head. James, of course, was dumbfounded.

"I realized I was hanging in the air about the time James dropped his stick and dropped to his knees. I had never seen anyone look so terrified. He was my friend. I didn't want to scare him. I landed and tried my best to explain what had happened. It took him a while to gather his wits, but he finally said, 'What are you?' In my haste to make it all make sense to him, I told him I was just a boy like him, and I must have been enchanted by garden fairies. He scoffed at that and said, 'I don't believe in fairies.' Without revealing too much, I explained that I was different, and I guess I must have told him that I would live a long time. When he grew up and wrote the story of Peter Pan, I think that was translated to being a boy who never grew up.

"James was not one to let a good story go to waste, and he told the others what he had witnessed. Most of them, fortunately, didn't believe him. He insisted that I show them. I refused for the longest time, but eventually, peer pressure became too much. One day, while we were all playing pirates in the garden, James chose me to be Peter again and immediately ran at me with a large fake sword. I saw the others looking at me and flew backward, up to the top of the garden wall. James was vindicated. The other boys were terrified. They dropped their sticks and ran away, screaming.

"I stood atop the wall staring at James. I was angry, and I screamed some very mean words at him. The next thing I know, I've got tears running down my face. I flew away into the woods, and I guess I stayed there for a couple of days. I was cold, wet, and hungry when Joseph, I mean, Uncle Joe, found me. I didn't know that Grandpa had sent him to Dumfries to keep an eye on me. When I didn't return, he cornered James and was told a wild story about a flying boy.

"Joe took me back to Wingfield Village, and I continued my education in more familiar surroundings. Eilie, I made a conscious decision to show off. I put my family at risk. If anyone had believed the boys, we could have all been exposed. Since no one would believe them, the boys eventually stopped telling the story. But James was a writer, even at fourteen. When he grew up, he became a successful writer. I didn't know that until decades later when I read a play written by JM Barrie."

"You were Peter Pan," Eilie said with wide eyes.

"No," Jake countered. "I was the apparent inspiration for Peter Pan. There is a big difference. My point for telling you this is to remind you how easy it is to let your guard down. In 1874 there were no cell phones with cameras. There was no internet where pictures could be posted. There weren't as many people to see you. You're going to have a much harder time keeping things hidden than I did. No matter how badly you want to tell someone or how good a friend you think they are, you cannot talk yourself into thinking it would be OK to tell or show anyone."

"I understand, Daddy," Eilie assured him. "It makes me sad I can't tell Francie, but I think it would freak her out if I did. I guess it would freak out anybody. I know why your friends ran away. I don't want to scare people. Scared people do dumb things because they stop thinking clearly. I promise I will never let anyone know."

"And we promise we will be here to help when you need us, Eilie," Jubal said. "You don't have to carry this burden alone. You can always talk to us if you feel overwhelmed."

"With you guys, I guess I have the best of both worlds," Eilie chuckled. "Hey, I finally understand what that means."

The men's laughter echoed off the hillside. "I think we have had enough flying for one day," Jubal said. "Let's get back to the house and rest up before supper."

"OK," Eilie said. "Daddy, can we go to Telluride tomorrow? I want to see it from the ground."

"Sure, why not?" Jake answered. "It's been years since I've walked around the town. I think you'll like the lift they have that goes up to Mountain Village. Do you want to go with us, Dad?"

"Not this time," Jubal said. "I have more to do before the Gathering. But I think my granddaughter and I can make a trip to town before you two head back to Tulsa. Would you like that, Eilie?"

"Very much, sir," she answered. "Last one to the barn is a rotten egg." She leaped off the ledge and dropped several feet before engaging her flight glands and gaining altitude. She headed toward the barn as fast as she could fly. Grinning, Jake shrugged his shoulders and dropped off the ledge. In a moment, he was parallel to the ground and took off after Eilie.

As Jubal lifted off and slowly began flying after them, he said, "Looks like I'm a rotten egg."

Chapter 10

Fears

Come to the edge. We might fall! Come to the edge. It's too high! COME TO THE EDGE! And they came. She pushed... And they flew.
- Christopher Logue

Tom Wingfield landed the Robinson 44 near Jubal's hangar at the Telluride Regional Airport. He switched off the engine and waited for the rotors to slow to a stop. "OK," he said. "Let's go warm up the old truck."

Tom, Eilie, and Jake exited the helicopter and walked toward the 1976 F150 parked inside the hangar. Tom got in on the driver's side and reached across to unlock the passenger door. Jake opened the door, and Eilie moved to the middle of the bench seat, resting her feet on the transmission hump in the middle of the floorboard. The men cranked down the windows, and Eilie marveled at the first manual windows she had ever seen. "How old is this truck?" she asked.

"More than forty years old," Jake answered.

"Where's the CD player?" Eilie asked as she examined the dashboard.

"CD player?" Jake said with a chuckle. "This doesn't even have a cassette player."

Eilie furrowed her brow. "What's a cassette?"

"Ancient technology," Tom replied. "This truck may be old, but she's reliable. I use her every time I come to town for supplies. We retired her as a ranch truck just two years ago. But she works just fine getting around town. And she's still got another ten years or more left in her."

"How come guys always call a machine a 'she' or 'her?'" Eilie asked.

Tom considered a couple of answers and then said, "I don't think I'm qualified to answer that question. How about you, Jake?"

"No, I'm going to pass on that one," he laughed. "Ask your mom when we get home."

Tom made clucking noises like a chicken and then started whistling as he put the truck into first gear and pulled out of the hangar. He pretended not to notice Jake glaring at him. Neither Tom nor Jake took much notice of the black SUV parked near the airport entry. Its windows were tinted black. And no one noticed the SUV as it followed slowly behind.

The trio made their way down Airport Road as it merged into Last Dollar Road. They got closer to the valley floor and pulled onto the 145 Spur. The road followed parallel to the

San Miguel River and became Colorado Avenue which splits Telluride north and south. Eilie was taking in all the sights along the route. "They have such cool buildings," she observed.

"Wait until we get to the middle of town," Tom said. "The buildings and houses get really cool then."

"Tom, I appreciate you showing us around," Jake said, "but I hope we're not keeping you from your duties at the ranch."

"I'm under orders to keep you two safe," he replied. "Besides, getting a day away from the ranch on a Monday is like a vacation. To tell the truth, I volunteered for this assignment. Jubal was going to send Bob and Carl as bodyguards, but I convinced him one of me was as good as two of them."

"Yeah, I seem to remember you had some special training in the Army," Jake said.

"Enough to stay out of trouble," he said, with a wink.

"What are we going to do first?" Eilie asked. "I want to see everything."

"I thought we'd spend the morning exploring Telluride and after lunch, we'll take the gondola up to Mountain Village," Jake offered.

"Is that like the one at the state fair back home?" Eilie asked.

"Sort of," Jake said. "But this one goes up the side of a mountain. In fact, it is the only free gondola public transportation system in North America."

"Can we go to McDonald's for lunch?" Eilie asked.

"Not in Telluride," Tom answered. "There is not a single chain restaurant anywhere in town. But I know a great place we can go to eat."

They drove through town on Colorado Avenue until they came to a parking area near the river. Tom pulled the truck into an off-street parking space near a footbridge crossing the river, parallel to the Maple Street Bridge that allowed vehicles to cross into the Telluride Town Park.

"Can't we drive into the park?" Eilie asked.

"Of course we can," Tom answered. "But it's more scenic to take the footpath over the river. The water is so clear, you can see the trout swimming."

"I expected to see more people here," Jake observed.

"It's still early in the day," Tom said. "The tourists will be out exploring in another hour or so. Before the day is over, they will be as thick as flies on watermelon."

The trio exited the truck and walked onto the footbridge. Eilie ran to the middle of the bridge, leaned over the railing, and scanned the rapidly flowing water for fish. "I see trout," she yelled out, pointing downward into the San Miguel River.

Jake and Tom caught up with Eilie, and they were all watching the Cutthroat trout move through the clear water. The bright red markings, which give the trout its name, were a sharp contrast to the mossy green of the rocks worn smooth by centuries of river flow.

"Isn't there a river that runs through Tulsa?" Tom asked.

"Yes," Eilie replied. "But it's a lot wider and a lot muddier."

"That's because the Arkansas River travels a long way to get to Tulsa," Jake explained. "Actually, it starts its journey toward Oklahoma right here in Colorado, near Leadville. It's as clear as this water when it starts, but by the time it gets to us, it's carrying a large amount of sand."

They heard a scream as a dark-haired woman came running up to Tom and grabbed his arms. "Please help me," she said with a French accent. "That man is trying to rob me." Tom instinctively moved the woman behind him as the man chasing her moved closer.

"Back off, buddy," Tom warned, as the man moved toward the center of the bridge. "We don't want any trouble. Why don't you just move along?" Tom readied himself for a fight in case the man got any closer. Suddenly, Tom's muscles tensed as 3 million volts of electricity coursed through him, and he fell in a heap on the wooden planks of the bridge deck. The woman was standing over him, holding a military-grade stun gun.

She turned to Jake and Eilie, who were still trying to understand what had happened. Eilie felt herself start to rise, but her dad held her firmly down. "No, no," said Anita Juneau. "You will both stay on the ground. If either of you tries to fly away, my friend here will do much more serious damage to your friend." The man stepped forward and pulled back his jacket to reveal a holstered handgun on his waist.

"What do you want?" Jake asked.

"It's quite simple really," Anita said. "I want you and your lovely daughter to follow me over to that car, and we will go for a short ride. We are not even going to leave town. My friend will stay here with your friend. When we get to where we are going, I will call him to let him know he can walk away. Eventually, your friend will wake up and be fine. If I do not call my friend in ten minutes and let him know you have been completely cooperative, he will have to use that nasty gun of his, and your friend will not be fine. I told you what I wanted was very simple. It only gets complicated if you choose to make it complicated."

"Daddy, I'm scared," Eilie said, almost without moving her lips.

"Take deep breaths," Jake said softly. "We're going to do what this woman wants." Jake still had his hands firmly on Eilie's shoulders. He turned her toward him and said, "Everything is going to be fine, Little. Trust me. Tom is going to be OK, and we are going to be OK." Eilie nodded at her dad and started breathing deeply so her ascendal glands would not kick in.

The henchman walked over to Eilie and her dad and pulled a cell phone from Jake's pocket. He went to Tom and propped him up against the bridge railing. He pulled the cell phone from Tom's shirt pocket and tossed both phones into the river. He then sat down beside Tom.

"My friend will keep your friend safe unless I say otherwise," Anita said.

She motioned toward the black SUV parked a few yards away. Jake moved Eilie toward the car and opened the back door for them. He kept his eyes firmly on Anita as she went around to the driver's door. When they were all in the vehicle, Jake asked, "Where are you taking us?"

"Not far, Darling," Anita answered. "I have someone very special I want you to meet. You two have so much in common. I am sure you will get along well."

Jake and Eilie were holding each other tightly in the back seat as the car made its way toward Shadow Lane. Jake's mind was in overdrive, trying to process everything that had happened in the last couple of days. *There has to be a Clan member behind this,* he thought to himself.

After a short drive on Shadow Lane, Anita parked the SUV in front of the old Victorian house. Crenshaw came out and opened the door for Jake and Eilie. Anita led the way up the stairs and through the front door as Crenshaw followed Eilie and Jake into the house. Eilie shivered when they entered the foyer, as if a cold hand had touched her shoulder. She sensed uneasiness, like the house was shrouded in misery.

Jake and Eilie were led into an interior room with no windows and only one door. It was too large to be a closet and too small to be a bedroom. There were two chairs set side-by-side and bolted to the floor. Handcuffs hung from each chair arm, and it was clear that the chairs were meant to keep them restrained. Crenshaw sat Jake and Eilie in the chairs and fastened the handcuffs to their wrists.

"Alright," Jake said to Anita, who was standing in the doorway. "You have us. Now make your call and tell your friend to walk away."

"But of course, Darling," she said. "I always keep my word." She called the guard and told him to come back to the house. "Now, as you are going to be our guests for the next few days, I suggest you make yourselves comfortable."

"This is hardly comfortable," Jake said with contempt. "Do you chain all your guests?"

"Only the extremely valuable ones," Anita shot back.

Dr. Geitzen entered the room, and Nurse Klipsch followed behind carrying a tray of syringes. The nurse placed the tray on a small table near the door. Geitzen walked over to Jake and proceeded to give him a cursory examination. He checked his eyes, ears, throat, and fingernails. Then he examined his head for cuts or bruises. "Everything seems fine," he said, as if talking to himself. He touched a digital thermometer to Jake's forehead. Geitzen then moved over to Eilie and began the same examination on her. Eilie cringed when he touched her, and Jake struggled to free himself. Crenshaw walked over and started to backhand Jake. Geitzen stopped him. "It is important he does not have any cuts or contusions," the doctor said.

Geitzen continued his examination of Eilie. "Everything is good," he muttered. He motioned to the nurse, and she took an empty syringe off the tray and approached Eilie. "My nurse will now take a small sample of your blood, young lady. We just need to run some tests."

The nurse put an elastic band around Eilie's arm to simplify finding a vein. Eilie clenched her teeth as the nurse inserted the needle and blood filled the syringe. She pulled the needle out quickly and unintentionally depressed the plunger. A stream of Eilie's blood shot into the air. All four of Connor's lackeys watched with their mouths open as the stream of blood simply floated in front of them. After a few seconds, the blood fell to the floor and splattered.

"Everything he told us is true," Geitzen said. "They are aliens."

"You bet I'm an alien, you jerk," Eilie yelled. "And if you don't let us go, I will fry your brains with my laser vision."

Anita clapped her hands. "A marvelous performance, dear girl. But, I have it on good authority that you do not have laser vision. However, I do admire your courage."

Geitzen walked to the tray and grabbed a syringe filled with a yellow liquid. He then walked over to Jake and inserted the needle into his arm. Jake immediately felt dizzy as the room seemed to spin. He slumped over in his chair, and Eilie screamed. "What did you do to my dad," she cried.

"Do not worry, young lady," Geitzen said coldly. "He is fine. He will sleep while we continue our tests. We cannot risk him flying away when we move him." He motioned for Crenshaw to remove the restraints. The henchman caught Jake as he began to fall to the floor. Another guard came in and helped carry Jake out of the room. The others filed out through the door, leaving Eilie alone.

Eilie fought with herself to keep her head clear. She wanted to cry and scream and shout, but she knew none of those things would solve the immediate problem or help her save her dad. And at this moment, she was squarely focused on protecting her dad. She was sure that Tom should be waking up any minute, and he would notify the police, who would search every house until they found her and her dad.

In fact, Tom was waking up. He was disoriented and having trouble getting his muscles to work. He called out, "Jake, Eilie." No response. *You idiot,* he thought to himself, *it was the woman. I shouldn't have turned my back on her.* He reached for his cell phone and realized they must have taken it. His first thought was to notify Jubal. But the more practical thing to do was to notify the town Marshal and call Jubal from there. Luckily, the Marshal's Office was just three blocks away.

Chapter 11

Accusations

*When once you have tasted flight, you will
forever walk the earth with your eyes turned
skyward, for there you have been, and there you
will always long to return. - Leonardo da Vinci*

Jake's head was spinning. He was trying desperately to
focus, but everything was distorted. He started taking
inventory of what he knew. He knew he was strapped down
to a bed or gurney. He could feel that his shirt was off, and
the room was cold. He could hear voices off in another
room, but he could not make out what they were saying.
He was aware of a bright light above him, but he could not
focus his eyes on anything. He decided that was what he
needed to concentrate on. He needed to focus his eyes on
one thing until he gained back control.

He turned his head to the left and could make out a
fuzzy square on the wall. It must be a picture frame. He
would bring that picture into focus. He struggled to get
his eye muscles to cooperate. Very slowly, the outline of

the frame became clearer, but he was still having difficulty with the picture in the frame. He tried to keep his eyes on a pinpoint spot, but they bounced around inside the frame. He closed his eyes and counted to twenty. Then he opened his eyes gradually so they would not be overwhelmed by too much light, too fast.

In the center of the frame, Jake saw a familiar sight. It was a photograph of the old Galloping Goose, the narrow gauge railcar that was used for years as the main transport around Telluride. He could even make out it was the Number 4, which was displayed on the west lawn of the Court House.

Now that he had better control of his eyes, he looked around the room. He was surrounded by equipment that belonged in a hospital. When he turned his head to the right, he saw a second operating table next to the one he was strapped to. He remembered his conversation with Gracie about organ transplants. He felt like he was waking up in a bad horror movie and any minute a hunchbacked Igor would come into the room followed by Dr. Frankenstein.

He heard a door open. Nurse Klipsch came in and placed a covered tray on a rolling cart. Jake raised his head and said, "Igor, I presume."

The nurse was not amused, but she fully understood his implication. She turned in a huff and left the room. Jake felt he was gaining back control of his muscles. He was able to move his toes and fingers with a bit of effort.

He had to figure a way out of his restraints and find Eilie. Desperation was setting in, and it was taking all his self-control not to panic.

He heard the door open again. This time the visitor was moving more slowly. Jake could not turn his head far enough to see who it was. Then, a figure moved into his line of sight. It was the oldest looking person Jake had ever seen. "Well, I suppose you are Dr. Frankenstein."

"Very amusing, Jacob," Connor said.

"Alright," Jake replied, "you know who I am, but I don't have a clue who you are."

"Do you mean you do not see the resemblance?" Connor asked. "No, I suppose not. Let me put it this way. Very soon you will look like I do. This is what you are destined to become, Brother."

"I know every member of the Clan," Jake answered. "You are not one of us."

"Oh, you think I called you brother in the general sense of the word," Connor snarled. "To the contrary, I was being very specific. I am your brother."

Jake was straining his neck, staring up at the old man. *He can't be serious,* he thought to himself. *I'm an only child.* "What are you talking about?" he demanded.

"Did Jubal never tell you?" Connor asked. "Dear old Dad never told you about your big brother? That's a bit dysfunctional, don't you think? Surely, our father would not keep anything this monumental from you. Dear me, I suppose the older Clan members never bothered to let you in on the joke. Not even the priest or the shepherd? How embarrassing."

"My mother only had one child," Jake said loudly.

"What a coincidence," Connor said. "So did mine. But my mother died 130 years before you were born. So we didn't have the same mother, you dolt. Did you really think Jubal had no life before you were born? Do you think he waited 350 years after crashing on this rock before he had a son?"

"What year were you born?" Jake demanded.

"1689," Connor answered. "I suppose that means I really am your *older* brother. What is that, about 170 years between us? Old Dad was quite the ladies' man."

"You're planning to steal my ascendal glands for yourself," Jake said. "There's something wrong with yours, and you need a transplant. Of course, you must have a compatible donor, a blood relative."

"Well, you're not as dumb as you look," Connor said in a snarky voice.

"Alright, listen," Jake said. "I'll make a deal with you. You can take my glands, and I won't fight you, but you have to let Eilie go. This does not concern her. It's between you and me. Let her go, please."

"How touching," Connor sneered. "But you see it does concern her. I can't just let her go. She'd be back here with the police before we even got started on the operation. Oh, and there is one other reason she has to stay. You see, if your glands don't function after the surgery, then I'm afraid I will have to use hers."

"You bastard!" Jake screamed. "You hurt her, and I will break your neck."

"Brother dear, haven't you noticed that you are not in control here?" Connor mocked.

"What happened to you?" Jake asked in a raspy voice. "How can you do this to a child, to family?

"You think your precious Clan is family?" Connor asked. "They are nothing but a bunch of inbred, crossbred half-breeds. They cower away from their gifts. We could have been gods to these puny humans. But what did Jubal have us do? He had us hide ourselves. He kept us in a tight little group instead of encouraging us to go to the four corners of the world and become conquerors and kings. We could be rulers now. We could be sitting in palaces around the globe. We could have armies at our command. But what are we? Engineers, librarians, professors, fry cooks, nurses, coaches, gardeners, and truck drivers. The Clan collectively sits on billions of dollars, yet individually they live the lives of paupers. And Jubal has set himself up as grand ruler of his thirty square mile kingdom."

"Jubal provides for every member of the Clan," Jake said in defense. "Anyone can have a scholarship or start a business, and Clan money is available. But being given everything means nothing. Each person has to earn their way, so they have self-worth and purpose."

"You really bought into the old con man's rhetoric, didn't you?" Connor retorted. "I suppose so. Look at you, the lowly college professor. Instead of teaching history, you could have made history. You could have been the history they write about. But instead, you write other people's histories. You are about to become a footnote of history, if anyone bothers to write the footnote."

"Why do you detest him?" Jake asked. "What did Jubal do to earn your hatred?"

Connor bent down over Jake until their noses were almost touching. He saw Jubal in Jake's eyes, and it enraged him. "What did he do to me?" he sputtered. "He made me old. He made me like this. He refused to cure me. He could have repaired my glands and made me whole again. Instead, he condemned me to be earthbound. He condemned me to be like a human."

"We're all part human," Jake responded. "I'm half-human just like you."

"I am not half-human!" Connor said, standing as tall as he could and looking at Jake with complete contempt. "My mother was from our homeworld. She was one of the original nine travelers. I may have been born on this miserable planet, but no human blood flows in my veins. You are the freak. You are the half-breed."

Jake was stunned. Why had his father kept all this from him? Why had he never mentioned a brother? He was feeling confused, betrayed, and foolish. Worse, he felt he had been lied to. If everything this madman said was true, then Jake had to doubt the validity of everything his father had told him. And it wasn't just Jubal who hid the truth. Matt and Joe had to know. They were there in the beginning, for the entire 350 years before Jake was born.

"What I am most looking forward to with new glands is renewed vigor," Connor said. "Your glands will restore me. I don't expect to reverse everything, but at least my death will be slowed. I expect I can gain another 2 or 3 hundred years. And I will no longer be earthbound. I have missed the rush of flight, the thrill of soaring. Please don't think I'm not grateful for your sacrifice. To show my gratitude, I will let you live. I don't have to worry about you running to the authorities of course because you would have to reveal too many family secrets to press charges against me. I don't think that would sit well with the Clan."

"You will not get away with this," Jake said with a strained voice.

"Oh, please," Connor said. "Don't be so melodramatic. I've gotten away with worse. Now, just be still for a while. We have at least two days of tests to finish before my surgeon will be ready. If you behave, I will have my men bring your daughter in, to keep you company. If you misbehave, I may have them lock her in a dark and cold basement." Connor locked the door as he left the room.

Tech Sergeant Carlos Sanchez sat nervously in the outer office of the Base Commander. He had a large file in his lap and was tapping it loudly with his fingers. Across the room, Tech Sergeant Sandy Bird was watching from his desk. As the clerk assigned to General Arthur Flagg's office, he had seen many nervous officers and non-coms sit in that same chair and sweat. It reminded him of high school when an errant student was waiting to see the principal.

"What are you so stressed about, Sanchez?" Sergeant Bird asked. "Did you get caught sleeping at your post?"

"You can't sleep on the Monitoring Floor," Sanchez answered. "There's always too much going on."

"Then why do you look like you're about to jump out of your skin?" Bird pressed.

"I can't tell you, Sandy," said Sanchez.

The phone on Sergeant Bird's desk buzzed. He answered it and said, "Yes, sir," before hanging up. He pointed his finger at the general's door and quietly said, "Good luck."

Sanchez rose from the chair, took a deep breath, and walked to the door. He stood in front of it for a moment before knocking. "Come in," came a voice from the other side. He entered the door and approached the general's desk, standing at attention with the folder under his arm.

General Flagg looked up and said, "At ease, Sergeant. What can I do for you?"

Sanchez relaxed his stance and said, "Sir, I believe I have troubling information regarding Colonel Wingfield. I realize I am going outside the chain of command, but I am concerned this could be a security risk, sir."

"Alright, you have my attention," the general said. "But, I give you fair warning, Sergeant. If you do not have solid evidence of a breach of conduct on the colonel's part, you will answer for a breach of conduct on your part. Is that understood?"

"Perfectly, sir," Sanchez answered.

Chapter 12

Freedoms

*I fly because it releases my mind
from the tyranny of petty things.*
- Antoine de Saint-Exupery

Tom Wingfield burst into the Marshal's Office on Spruce Street. "Hoyt," he yelled into the group of people behind the front counter. "There's been a kidnapping. We need to call Jubal."

Marshal Hoyt Kendrick rose from his desk and moved toward Tom. He looked every bit the part of a western marshal. He was tall, lean, and wore a mustache that could have easily been confused with a shaving brush. His attire was reminiscent of an Old West lawman. A cowboy hat was on a wall hook behind his desk. He proudly did his part to represent his town to the tourists.

"Tell me exactly what you're talking about, Tom," Marshal Kendrick said. "What happened?"

"Jake and his daughter, Eilie, were taken by a couple of outsiders," Tom said. He went into great detail describing the two assailants, and embarrassingly explained how he was duped by a pretty lady.

The Marshal went to his desk, strapped on his gun belt, and grabbed his hat. He stopped at his dispatcher's desk and said, "Mary, get a-hold of the airport and tell them not to let any planes leave until they hear from me. And call the chief up at Mountain Village." He turned to Tom and pointed at his desk, "You call Jubal and let him know what's happened." He then turned to his deputy and said, "Pete, gather the boys and put up a roadblock at each end of town. Check every car leaving. We all know what Jake looks like. Let's see if we can come up with a recent picture of his daughter. Come on; let's go find 'em."

As the Marshal and his deputies were leaving, Tom called the ranch. Gracie answered the phone, and he explained what had happened and that they needed a picture of Eilie. Immediately, Gracie forwarded a photo of Eilie and Jake to the cell phones of every law enforcement officer in San Miguel County. She also sent one to Mary and manipulated the caller ID so it would look like Mary was the one who sent them.

Jubal picked up an extension at Gracie's prompting, and Tom filled him in on the details. "Alright, Joe and I will be there as soon as we can get the other chopper airborne. Meet us at the airport with the truck." Jubal then called Joe to meet him at the ranch hangar. "Gracie," he said, "you know what to do."

"Yes, Jubal, I am already on it," she responded. "And, Jubal, I have the identity of our spy."

Eilie was trying very hard to squeeze her hands out of the handcuffs. She had bright red circles around her wrists as proof of her efforts. There was enough chain on each pair to almost allow her to bring her hands together. She was worried about her dad. She felt that Tom would be OK because she knew he was young and very strong, but she worried about her dad. And now that she knew how old he really was, she was even more concerned about what had been done to him.

She felt a sharp pain in her left wrist, like an electrical shock. *My wrist can't be hurting again,* she thought. She looked at the bracelet her grandpa had given her and blinked her eyes. It seemed as if the wings on the bracelet were glowing. Then she heard something, like a voice off in the distance. Suddenly, the voice was in her head. "Eilie, can you hear me?" She looked all around the room and even behind her. No one was there.

"Eilie, can you hear me?"

"Who's there?" she asked, feeling very confused.

"It's Gracie," the voice said. "Can you hear me?"

"Where are you?" Eilie asked. "You sound like you're in my head."

"I am," Gracie said. "But not directly. You can hear me through the bracelet. I have activated the GPS and pinpointed your location. Help will be arriving soon."

"But how can I hear you in my head if you're talking through the bracelet?" she asked.

"It has to do with nanotechnology and nerve integration circuits," Gracie answered. "But right now, I need you to help me help you and your dad."

"They took Daddy to another room, and I don't know what they're doing to him," she said.

"Are you alone?" Gracie asked

"Yes," Eilie answered.

"Is there a computer anywhere in the room with you?" Gracie asked.

"There's a laptop on a table by the door," Eilie reported

"Good. Get over to the computer," Gracie prompted

"I can't. I'm handcuffed to a chair that's stuck to the floor," Eilie said in frustration.

"OK. Let's deal with the handcuffs first," Gracie began. "Lift up your right arm, so the chain of the handcuff is between your arm and the chair. Now, look at your bracelet. Do you see the red dot appearing below the center pair of wings?"

"Yes, I see it," Eilie answered.

"Turn your wrist, so the dot is pointing at the chain like a laser pointer," Gracie instructed.

Eilie turned her left arm until a red dot appeared on the handcuff chain. "It's on the middle link," she said.

"Good. Hold still," Gracie said. The laser pointer suddenly got very bright and the next thing Eilie knew the chain-link was cut in half. Her right arm was free. "Don't let the end of the chain touch your skin. It might burn. Now, remove your bracelet and let's do the same thing to the other chain."

Eilie did as Gracie instructed, and she was quickly free of the chair. She ran over to the computer by the door. "I'm at the computer. What do I do now?"

"Lay the bracelet face-down on the touchpad of the computer," Gracie said calmly.

"OK. It's there. What will that do?" Eilie asked.

"I am taking control of this computer, and through it, I can operate all their security systems," Gracie explained. "Only one of the computers in this house is connected to the internet, but all the rest are connected to each other. I see you now, Eilie. There is a camera above the door. I am sending a video loop to the camera from a half-hour ago. If anyone looks at a monitor, they will think you are still sitting in the chair."

"Can you see Daddy?" Eilie pleaded.

"Yes," Gracie answered. "He is in what appears to be an operating room, just two rooms away from you. Eilie, a lot of police cars are approaching the house. They are staying out of sight, so the people inside don't get scared and try to hurt you and your dad. Since I have control of their computers now, I can guide you toward your dad, so you can use the bracelet to free him. I will see what's really happening through the security cameras, but they will see what I want them to see. I know where every person in the house is, and I can get you to your dad without being seen."

"OK, Gracie, let's get Daddy." Eilie was energized and determined to reunite with her father.

"Good. The door has a magnetic lock. When you hear it click, open the door." The lock clicked, and Eilie opened the door, cautiously looking into the hall. "It's OK," Gracie said. "Everyone is busy and won't see you. Go left to the second door down the hall."

Eilie moved to the door and heard a click as Gracie turned off the magnetic lock. She quickly entered the room and closed the door behind her. She ran over to her dad lying on the table and threw her arms around his neck. "Are you OK, Daddy?" she asked as she squeezed him tightly.

"Eilie, how did you get in here?" Jake asked in amazement.

"I'll tell you in a minute," she said. "OK, I'm holding the bracelet at the strap. Zap it."

"Who are you talking to?" Jake asked.

"Gracie," Eilie answered. "She's in my head." She moved around the table and cut through the straps on Jake's arms and legs.

Jake tried to jump off the table, but was still weak from the drugs he had been given. He wrapped his arms around Eilie and hugged her like he had never hugged her before.

"Eilie," Gracie said, "my connection with you will break in just a few minutes. Your antibodies are attacking the nanobots, and they will be useless. So before I lose you, this is what I want you to do." Eilie listened intently as Gracie explained what was about to happen.

"OK, Daddy," Eilie said. "We need to wait here by the door."

"What are we waiting for?" Jake asked as he was putting his shirt on.

Five car alarms went off simultaneously outside the old Victorian house on Shadow Lane. "That," Eilie said.

Crenshaw, the five armed guards, and Anita Juneau all ran out of the house toward the ringing cars with keys in hand. Suddenly, twenty-five law enforcement officers moved in from behind and around those cars with guns drawn. The criminals moved their arms into the air in unison. Eilie and Jake made their way out the back door where Jubal and Joe were waiting for them. They pointed toward the old truck where Tom was standing. Eilie ran down the steps and hugged Tom, relieved he was OK.

The Telluride deputies, Mountain Village police officers, and San Miguel County Sheriff's deputies converged on the overwhelmed menagerie of confused criminals and quickly disarmed and restrained each of them. Marshal Kendrick walked up to Anita and took her car keys. "I don't think you're going anywhere, Miss Juneau," he said. "But I will be happy to escort you to my office until our friends from Interpol get to Denver. It seems they want to have a conversation with you about some parking tickets." He took her by the arm and moved her toward his truck.

"Officer, Darling," Anita said. "I think there is something you should know about the people who were in that house."

"Alright," Marshal Kendrick said. "What should I know?" He turned her around and cuffed her hands behind her back, guiding her into the back seat.

"They are aliens," Anita said in a whisper. "All of the ones named Wingfield, even the old man. They are aliens."

"Is that so?" he asked.

Anita looked down at the marshal's boots and saw that he was floating about five inches off the pavement. "You are a Wingfield," she said with a gasp.

Marshal Kendrick touched the wide brim of his cowboy hat and gave a nod. "On my mother's side, Ma'am." He shut the truck door and headed toward the house.

Eilie and Jake were watching as Geitzen and his nurse were being handcuffed and placed into a car. Joe and Jubal were coming out of the house with Connor, each holding an arm to help him down the steps. They opened the door of the old truck, and Connor got in and moved to the middle of the seat.

"Isn't he going with the police?' Jake asked.

Jubal placed his hand on Jake's shoulder. Jake could see redness in his father's eyes and realized he was fighting back tears. "No, son," Jubal said. "He is dying. He's coming to Tutela to die with family."

"Do you know what he tried to do to me?" Jake asked incredulously.

"Yes, and I don't expect you to forgive him," Jubal answered. "I don't expect you to forgive me. But he will not die alone in a jail cell."

Marshal Kendrick walked up to Jubal. "We've got all nine of them secured. Gracie was able to ID each one from the security cameras inside the house. The whole lot of them has a pile of warrants from all over. The county boys will take Kendrick and his crew. I'll hold the doctor and nurse and the Frenchie for the Euro-cops. I can deliver them to the Interpol agents when they get to Denver. There's no way they would ever find their way to Telluride. I will take each of your statements later."

"Thanks for everything, Hoyt," Jubal said. "You'll be at the Gathering?"

"Wouldn't miss it for the world," Marshal Kendrick said. He tipped his hat to Eilie and added, "And it is a pleasure to meet you, Cousin Eilie. I can't wait to see you fly."

"I didn't know I had so many cousins," Eilie said.

The Marshal knelt in front of Eilie and took a handcuff key from his vest pocket. He gently removed the handcuffs from her. He looked at the bruising and red marks on her wrists and said, "Gracie sent me a text explaining how you rescued your dad. That was a mighty brave thing you did. Now, I don't know if Jubal has told you about the long list of responsibilities you have as a Fledgling, but one of the big ones is protecting the Clan. You did that today. And as Marshal of Telluride, Colorado, I hereby deputize you as an honorary member of the Marshal's Posse." He removed his star and pinned it on Eilie's shirt.

Eilie smiled and, for the first time in three days, felt at ease. Her dad was safe, Tom was unhurt, and all the bad guys were going to jail. She felt like she had suddenly become part of something really big. She wasn't afraid anymore. In fact, she was feeling exceptionally courageous. The only thing she could not figure out, was who the old man was sitting in the truck. "Thank you," she said to the Marshal.

Tom lowered the tailgate and climbed into the bed of the truck. He reached for Eilie's hand and pulled her up. Jake climbed in, and they each found a spot to sit for the drive to the airport. There would be another day to tour the town.

Chapter 13

Confrontations

Keep thy airspeed up, lest the earth come up and smite thee. - William Kershner

After Tom and Joe landed the two helicopters close to the hangar, the two men busied themselves getting Connor into a Jeep for the drive up to the house. Jake was still hesitant to be around Connor. He said he would walk to the house with Eilie since the Jeep was full. Eilie and Jake began the hike to the house, and she asked, "Who is that man, Daddy?"

"It seems he is my brother," Jake answered.

"You didn't know you had a brother?" she asked.

"No, I didn't know," he said.

"You don't sound happy about it," Eilie said. "I would be happy if I found out I had a brother."

"Yeah, well..." Jake couldn't finish his thought.

"I think you want to be alone right now," Eilie suggested. "Is it OK if I fly the rest of the way to the house? I have some questions I want to ask Gracie."

Jake smiled. "Sure, Honey. Go ahead."

"Everything is going to be OK, Daddy. Don't worry so much." She made herself airborne and kissed her dad on the cheek. Then she made a beeline for the porch. She landed just as she touched the handle of the front door. Once she cleared the threshold, she ran straight to the study and cautiously peeked in to make sure no one was there.

"Gracie?" Eilie called out. "Can I see you?"

Gracie materialized in the middle of the room. "Hello, Eilie. How are you feeling?"

"That's what I wanted to talk about," she said. "I'm feeling different. I don't know how to describe it except 'different.' What's happening to me?"

"You are feeling a little more grown up," Gracie answered. "What you went through today allowed you to stretch your wings. You found yourself in a situation where you could not be a helpless child waiting for an adult to rescue you. You had to assume an adult role. Your dad needed your help, and you rose to the task. You thought about someone else's needs and put another person's safety above your own."

"But you helped me," Eilie said. "I didn't do any of that by myself. You made it where I could hear you, and you showed me how to free my dad. I couldn't have done that without you."

"I only did what I was programmed to do," Gracie explained. "I was simply the tool you used to free your dad and yourself. I told you when we first met that as long as you wear that bracelet, you carry my wings. The bracelet allows me to fly with you, to connect to you in an emergency. Jubal designed the bracelet to provide you a link to me so I could serve you as you need. Once I was informed you were in danger, I used the bracelet to determine your location, and I activated the automatic nano neural-transmitters so we could communicate. All that did was inject nanobots into your nervous system. You probably felt a mild shock when it happened."

"Oh I felt it, alright," Eilie said. "But what are nanobots?"

"They are tiny machines no larger than a molecule, she explained. Once they were injected, the nanobots traveled your circulatory system and set up a link in your auditory nerves so you could hear me. After that, it was just a matter of showing you how to use the various tools built into the bracelet. But the system has one flaw we cannot overcome. Your autoimmune system, which attacks germs or viruses and keeps you well, will also attack the nanobots. So, we only had a few minutes before communication was lost. I can still monitor you through the bracelet, but you can't hear me once your body destroys the nanobots."

"How many tools are in the bracelet?" Eilie asked.

"I could print out the instruction manual for you," Gracie said. "It's 107 pages."

"Maybe later," Eilie said. "But I still don't understand why I feel this way."

"Eilie, you are growing up," Gracie said in a soft voice. "Today you got a taste of adult responsibility. You momentarily saw the world through a different lens."

"My dad is really sad right now," Eilie intoned. "He just discovered he has a brother, but he is not happy about it. Why?"

"Have a seat, Eilie," Gracie said, motioning to a chair. "This might take a while to explain. Your father learned some things today that tore at the very foundation of who he thought he was. He had always thought of himself as an only child. He had a clear picture of his place in the family and in the world. Learning that he had a brother meant that he did not fully know what had happened before his own birth. You see, people tend to view the world only from the point of their entry. Most never consider what happened before they were born. Humans especially create an almost magical celebration centered on their date of birth. It is a major focus for children and continues into adulthood. Each person's identity is invested in the significance of their particular birthday.

"Several different realities became shifted from your dad's perspective when he learned about Connor Wingfield. Probably the most troubling shift was realizing that his father had not been completely honest with him. Jubal had kept Connor's existence a secret from Jake. Connor was an extremely troubled person. He harbored hostility and resentment toward others, especially Jubal. He would not abide by Clan rules to keep his ability to fly from outsiders. He enjoyed shocking and frightening others into believing he was a wizard or a demon. Eventually, for the good of the Clan, Jubal was forced to ban Connor from the protection of the Clan. By the time Jake was born, Connor was only a memory. No one was even certain if he was still alive."

"Why is he older than Grandpa?" Eilie asked.

"He looks older because he accelerated his own aging by abusing his ascendal glands," Gracie answered. "Connor allowed himself to become addicted to flying. It became an obsession. For him, it was the only thing he had that set him apart from others. It was his only identity. He felt it made him superior. Sadly, his feelings of inadequacy came with a price. His body is shutting down from years of overindulgence."

"So, because he thought he had to prove he was better than others, he actually proved he wasn't," Eilie reasoned.

"Exactly, my dear girl," Gracie said. "Pride combined with hate is a dangerous mixture. And because he was addicted to ascendaline, he was willing to do anything to get another dose of it, even if it meant forcefully taking it from his brother, or you."

"What can I do to make my dad feel better?" she asked.

"Remind him you still need him," Gracie answered. "You always will need him. But as you get older and more mature, you won't need him for the same reasons. It is normal for children to pull away from their parents as they get older.

But don't let your need to gain your independence be the cause to push away the very people who help you become independent."

"After all the trouble Connor caused, why did Grandpa bring him back to the ranch?" Eilie asked.

"Despite Connor's limited ability to love," Gracie said, "he is still loved by others; particularly by Jubal. There are bad guys, and there are good guys. And sometimes there are people who are both. Sometimes, the only thing that keeps a person from becoming completely bad is the fact that someone loves them."

"What will happen to him?" she asked.

"Jubal will look after him and try to make him as comfortable as possible until he dies," Gracie said. "Then, he will be buried in the family cemetery on the other side of the ridge. He will be mourned, and he will be missed. He will be remembered. Eventually, the number of good memories will become greater than the number of bad memories."

"I feel cheated," Eilie said.

"In what way?" Gracie asked.

"I have Uncle Joe and Uncle Matt who really aren't my uncles," she said. "I had Uncle Jubal, who really is my grandpa. My only real uncle is Connor, and I never got to know him as an uncle."

"There is still time," Gracie nudged.

Colonel Charles Wingfield walked into the office of General Arthur Flagg at the NORAD Complex. The general looked up from his desk and said, "Ah, Charlie. Come on in."

"You sent for me, sir?" the colonel asked.

"Yes, please. Have a seat," the general said, motioning to a chair.

Colonel Wingfield sat in the chair and felt uneasiness in the pit of his stomach. He knew the general only asked someone to sit if there was a serious matter to discuss.

"Charlie, a man on your floor has brought something to my attention that needs some explanation," the general began. "I thought you and I could discuss it before it becomes a formal inquiry. I have interviewed this man myself, and I don't mind telling you that, at first, I thought he was a quack. But he has presented some pretty damning evidence to support his claim."

"What is his claim, sir?" the colonel asked.

"He thinks you are covering up proof that the Black Knight has been transmitting," General Flagg said. "He says he has intercepted transmissions from the satellite and presented proof to you. He also says you instructed him to ignore any future transmissions."

"We must be talking about Tech Sergeant Sanchez," the colonel said. "Yes, his wave monitor did indicate that a transmission may have come from that piece of space junk. But, I was able to determine that it was an echo from another satellite."

"Sergeant Sanchez showed me wave charts that indicated a definite transmission from the Black Knight," the general countered. "He ran several signal analysis programs and got the same answer each time."

"I don't know how to explain that, sir," Charlie responded. "But I assure you there is a logical explanation."

"I hope so, Charlie," General Flagg said. "Don't get me wrong. I don't think you're an alien spy in disguise. But if that blasted contraption is transmitting, I want to know what it is. It has been a thorn in our side for way too long. We know more about Russian satellites than we do about that thing. Our job is to monitor everything overhead. We can't ignore it until we are completely certain it is not a threat. If we determine it is a threat, we will take appropriate measures."

"I will personally run a signal analysis from the time Sergeant Sanchez received the first alarm," Charlie assured him.

"I have ordered Major Westin to run the analysis," the general said. "It's nothing personal, Charlie. But I have to cover my bases. The only way to clear you of any wrongdoing is to have someone besides you or the sergeant check out everything."

"Am I relieved of duty, sir?" the colonel asked.

"Not at all," General Flagg answered. "Carry on with your usual duties. I am reassigning Sergeant Sanchez to another department until this is settled. I don't want his presence on your floor to cause you any discomfort. I will confer with you when Major Westin has completed his analysis. I want to get this cleared up as soon as possible with the least disruption."

～

Jake had showered to remove the sweat of his ordeal on Shadow Lane. He realized that the shower was probably more symbolic than substantial. But still, he felt better for having done it and was buttoning a clean shirt when there was a knock on his door. "Come in," he yelled at the door.

Jubal stepped into the room. He closed the door behind him and stood quietly looking at Jake. "I suppose you don't want to see me right now," he finally said.

"I don't know what I want right now, Dad," Jake said with a sigh.

"You have every right to be angry. Particularly, with me," Jubal said.

Jake sat on the edge of his bed and buried his face in his hands. He was trying to choose the right starting point for what he wanted to say. There were so many feelings in him fighting to get out. He wanted to lash out at his father. He wanted to go into the other room where his kidnapper was resting and tear into him. He wanted to take Eilie and go back to Tulsa. He wasn't sure he could face any of the Clan. He looked up at Jubal and said, "You don't trust me."

"Why do you say that?" Jubal asked. "Of course I trust you."

"No, you don't," Jake snapped. "You haven't trusted me since Dumfries. And apparently, you didn't trust me before. I have a brother, and you didn't trust me enough to tell me."

"If anything, I didn't trust him," Jubal rebutted. "You have no idea what horrible things your brother put me through, what he put the Clan through. Do you know how much a failure I felt as a father? Connor was long out of our lives before you came along. I was determined to not make the same mistakes with you. Why do you think I was so hard on you as a boy? I didn't want you to turn out like him. And thankfully, you didn't. It's not that I didn't trust you, Jake. I didn't trust myself. I doubted my own ability to raise a boy to be a decent man. You are a decent man. And you are a much better father than I was."

"That monster down the hall was going to remove my glands surgically. And if that failed, he was going to take Eilie's. He was going to cut into your granddaughter. And you bring him here like he is a prodigal son. Aren't you just a little disgusted by that?"

"More than you can know. But he is my son. For over 250 years, I was not even sure if he was alive. I sent people out across Europe looking for him. I lay awake at night for decades feeling I had failed him. It took having you to show me that I wasn't a failure as a father. I now know that the sole burden of responsibility rests squarely on his shoulders. He chose to be what he was. By the time I came to understand that, there was no point in telling you about him. I didn't want you to build him up in your imagination as some heroic figure you needed to find and rescue. Or worse, to emulate."

"There is no way you can justify allowing that maniac to be in the same house as your granddaughter. At least put him in one of the cabins away from the house. You won't even need to put a guard on him. If he tries to escape, he'll just die in the woods."

"Jake, he is almost dead already. I respect your position, and I understand your anger. But I'm asking you to understand my dilemma. He is being punished for his crimes. He is his own executioner. Let me have him for his last days. Let me at least try to remember how he used to be."

"I am not letting him off that easy," Jake said as he stormed out of the room and headed down the hall to the room Connor was using.

"Son, don't," Jubal pleaded, following after him.

Jake threw open the door and stopped in his tracks at the sight that greeted him. Connor was sitting up in bed, smiling. In a chair next to the bed, Eilie was laughing. "Hi, Daddy," she said. "Uncle Connor was just telling me about his first flight as a Fledgling. It's really funny."

"Eilie, get away from him!" Jake said almost in a panic.

Eilie rose from the chair and went to her father. She took his hand and looked up at him. "It's OK, Daddy. I have forgiven him. And he apologized to me. He told me he wants to apologize to you. It would mean a lot to me if you let him. Please."

Jake was in shock. He could think of no rebuttal to what Eilie said. He felt his anger subside and he felt a wave of emotion overtake him as tears rolled down his cheeks. He began to tremble; not in fear or anger, but just from the sheer release of emotion. Eilie was still holding his hand as she led him over to the bedside chair and sat him down. "Daddy, I would like you to meet your big brother, Connor. Uncle Connor, I would like you to meet your little brother, Jacob." She leaned forward between them and said, "This is the part where you shake hands."

The two men stared at each other for a moment, and then simultaneously reached out their hands in a clasp that seemed to span the centuries. Eilie looked at Connor and saw that he was crying too. She went to the nightstand on the other side of the bed and retrieved a box of tissue, which she placed between them. When she looked up at her grandfather, she saw that he had tears streaming down his face as well. She grabbed two tissues and went to Jubal. As she handed him the tissue, she said, "Let's go downstairs and talk. I want to find out more about this long list of responsibilities Fledglings have."

Jubal wiped his eyes and put his arm around Eilie. Heading for the door, he said, "There isn't a single one you can't handle."

Chapter 14

Healings

I have often said that the lure of flying is the lure of beauty. The reason flyers fly, whether they know it or not, is the aesthetic appeal of flying.
- Amelia Earhart

Members of the Clan had been arriving for three days. Half of them drove, and Tom had been busy making sure everyone was parking in the appropriate places. Joe had been shuttling people from the airport in the helicopter. Open-top jeeps, four-wheelers, and golf carts were filled to capacity as the visiting family was touring the ranch and taking in the mountain air. The small children were enjoying the 'petting zoo' Tom and Eilie had put together with some recently birthed kids, lambs, and piglets. Older boys were catching trout in the stream while Matt was explaining the finer points of fly casting.

Eilie was having girl talk with three cousins from Texas and South Carolina. She learned there was a fourth girl who would be arriving soon from Arkansas. It was refreshing for her to have girls to talk to. The last few days, she had been surrounded by men. The girls compared birthdays and found that they had all been born within six months of each other. They loved Eilie's bracelet and said they would ask their parents to order one online for them too.

Katie Wingfield had bright red hair, lived in Dallas, was the oldest of the group, and the most talkative. Eilie didn't mind that she dominated the conversation, but it would be nice to learn more about her other cousins. Mattie Wingfield was the one from South Carolina, and Eilie thought she had the coolest accent. Then, there was Courtney Butler from Galveston. She had very blonde hair, which Eilie thought might be from too much time on the beach. The cousin, who had not arrived yet, Holly Wingfield, would be coming from Hot Springs, and Eilie was eager to meet her because she was also taking ballet lessons.

Eilie had learned a phrase that the flyers used to acknowledge each other. She would not initiate it because she wasn't sure yet who all the flyers were. But she would respond in kind when she heard 'Clear skies, Cousin.'

Feeding over a hundred people was a logistical nightmare, but Jubal had every detail planned out. The Hotel kitchen had been fully stocked, and a few of the adults had volunteered to help Cousin Paul, a chef in a four-star New York hotel, prepare several meals. Friday night, a real chuck wagon prepared the evening meal, and everyone ate outside while watching a huge bonfire. The ranch staff was ready for everything. A few people even asked if they could book their next vacation at Jubal's resort.

An excursion to Telluride and Mountain Village was planned for Saturday. A tour bus was scheduled to pick up the non-flying adults and the children at 9 AM. Eilie explained to her girl cousins that she couldn't go on the tour because she was helping her dad care for the elderly visitor who was staying at the ranch for a few days. She did not like being dishonest, but she also knew that the odds were good that those same cousins might find themselves flying in about ten years, and she would help them adjust to their new responsibilities in the family.

Most of the Clan was being housed in the Hotel about a hundred yards from the main house. The top two floors literally were set up like a hotel with guest rooms on either side of a long hallway. The ground floor was a huge meeting hall where everyone could eat. The kitchen was to the back, and family members would take turns preparing the meals. The far end of the meeting hall was set up as a game room with pool tables, foosball, pinball, and a host of other amusements, including a 1955 Wurlitzer jukebox with original 45 RPM records.

While walking through the Hotel, Eilie noticed that the elevator had a button for a basement. She tried it, but could not get it to work. So she went to the stairwell and tried to go down the stairs to the basement. The doors were locked. She made a mental note to ask her grandpa about it after the Gathering. As she was leaving, she thought she heard a voice and turned back toward the stairwell. The sound stopped, and she decided she was imagining things, or maybe it was just an echo.

Eilie was learning the names of visiting family members. She found it a little disconcerting that most of the adults knew who she was and that she was a Fledgling. Her dad explained to her that it had been a very long time since the last Fledgling, and that she was a big celebrity for the Clan. That made her a bit self-conscious. She wasn't really sure she wanted so much attention.

Above all the excitement and activity of the Gathering, Eilie was most looking forward to Saturday when all the flyers would gather in the east meadows and fly together. She could not imagine what it would look like for fifty-six people to fly at once. The ranch hands had set up some chairs for a handful of observers who would not be flying. That would, of course, include Matt, Joe, and Tom. Most of all, Eilie wanted Connor to sit with them. Now that her dad had made peace with his brother, she thought it would be nice to invite him to watch.

She had brought some soup to Connor on Friday after the chuck wagon dinner and told him of her idea. He did not think the rest of the Clan would approve. "You're young, and you don't know the bad history I have with some of the older members," Connor told her. "I left the Clan on very bad terms."

"But Daddy and Grandpa forgave you," Eilie said. "Why shouldn't everyone else?"

"Everyone else is not a direct blood relative," Connor reminded her. "The others may not be as forgiving. I don't want to ruin your first Soaring Ceremony by making some people uncomfortable. Thank you for caring. But we should let sleeping dogs lie."

"If the others say it's OK, will you join us," she prodded.

Connor laughed out loud and said, "Alright, but if one person says 'no,' then I want you to drop it. Agreed?"

Eilie agreed and began to formulate a plan to get all the flyers to invite Connor. She had less than sixteen hours to pull it off. She sat with Connor while he ate and asked, "What's it like to be over 300 years old?"

"The time goes by faster than you would think," he said with a little hesitation. "I just wish I was in better health to enjoy it."

"I'm sorry things have turned out so bad for you," Eilie said. "I wish I could do something to make it better."

"Yeah, I'm sorry too," Connor said as he set his soup down. "Let me tell you something, young lady. Don't make the mistakes I have made. Don't confuse pride with stupidity. I have been stupid. I allowed myself to believe that I didn't need direction. I wanted to go wherever the wind blew me. I spent so much time flying higher and higher, that I didn't realize I was getting older and older. I didn't learn the lesson of Icarus."

"Who is Icarus?" Eilie asked.

Connor stared at Eilie in disbelief. "Haven't you learned the story in school? How old are you?"

"I'm ten," Eilie said.

"You seem older than ten," he said. "And you're a Fledgling?"

Eilie nodded her head.

"Well, let me tell you the lesson of Icarus," Connor said, leaning forward. "And pay attention. Maybe you won't throw away your life like I have. There was a Greek craftsman named Daedalus who could build anything. He decided he wanted to escape the city of Athens and take his son, Icarus, with him. He built two sets of wings made of feathers and wax. He instructed Icarus to follow him as they made their escape. Icarus put on his wings and flew into the sky. He fell in love with flying and soared higher and higher. His father warned him to not fly too close to the sun because the heat would melt the wax and the wings would fall apart and be useless. Icarus did not listen to his father and flew toward the sun. As Daedalus warned, the wax melted, and the feathers fell out of the wings. Without the wings to hold him up, Icarus fell into the sea and drowned. I am Icarus. Or rather, I am as foolish as Icarus. I did not listen to my father. My wings have melted, and I am falling into the sea. Soon, I will drown."

"I won't fly too high, or too fast, or too often, Uncle Connor," she said. "And I do listen to my father, and yours.

I wish I could put the feathers back in your wings so you could fly with us tomorrow."

"You are a sweet child," he said. "Try to stay the way you are. Don't let life talk you into being anything less than the wonderfully beautiful person you are."

"What did you do when you left home way back then?" Eilie asked. "You were all alone, weren't you?"

"Yes, I was very alone," Connor answered. "I had to get by on my wits. I used my ability to fly to fool people and take their money. I would pretend to be a shaman or an Indian guru. People love a good magic show, and I made a lot of money pretending to be a magician. I would set up a tent and charge admission. I learned a few sleight-of-hand tricks to whet their appetites, and then I would perform my grand finale by levitating above their heads. Some ladies actually fainted. To prevent a complete riot, I always had wires rigged backstage to let them think I performed a simple illusion. The only way to really perform an illusion is to make it real."

"I bet you had some really exciting times," Eilie said. "It would be fun to do stuff like that."

"I'll tell you where the real fun is, Fledgling," he snapped. "You stay with family. Don't go off on some fool's journey looking for greener grass or fame and fortune. Stay true to yourself and true to your birthright. You are a child of the stars. You may never get to see our homeworld, but you are still a child of the stars."

"Uncle Connor," Eilie said, standing up, "I have seen my homeworld. Earth is my home. And it's the home of our whole family now. We don't need to look for a brighter star than the one that we see every day. I can be a child of the stars and never travel further than the treetops. I am a Wingfield, and I think I have the best family ever. I could never leave all these wonderful people. I think you're wonderful, too. I will be sad when you're gone."

Connors eyes filled with tears. Eilie walked over to him and hugged him tightly.

"Thank you, dear girl," Connor said almost in a sob. "You cannot know how much you have softened a hard heart. I think I am no longer afraid. And I owe that to you."

Eilie pulled back from the hug and looked into the old man's eyes. They seemed a little kinder, a little younger. She smiled at him and kissed him on the cheek. "I need to go now. I have to get everything ready, so you can watch the Soaring tomorrow."

Connor nodded his head. "Remember what I said. If one person objects to me being there, I will stay here in this room. Agreed?"

"Agreed, sir," Eilie acknowledged, closing the bedroom door behind her.

⤚

The day of the Soaring was here. The busload of non-participants was on its way to Telluride. The viewing seats were placed on top of the portable stage. Jubal had a microphone and speakers set up to the far left side of the stage so he could address the crowd. He would make his usual speech about the strength of family and the importance of unity. Then, he would introduce Eilie to the Clan as their newest Fledgling and have her lead everyone in the Soaring Ceremony.

It took about a half hour for all the Clan members to arrive at the staging area. The crowd took a leisurely walk because no one wanted to be too tired to fly. Jubal was taking a head count when he realized he could not see Eilie, Jake, or Joe. He was about to call everyone to order when a Jeep came into the meadow carrying four people. Jubal saw the missing three, and Connor was with them.

Jake and Joe helped Connor out of the jeep and onto the stage. Eilie was carrying a clipboard and a pen. She motioned for Jubal to come to the edge of the stage. "Eilie, what's going on?" he asked. "Connor said he didn't want to be here for the Soaring. That he was too embarrassed to be around any of the Clan."

"He made a deal with me that if I could get everyone to say it was OK, then he would come," she said. "And he said if even one person said no, then he would stay at the house." She handed Jubal the clipboard. At the top of a sheet of paper he read; *We, the undersigned, wish Connor Wingfield to attend the Soaring Ceremony at the Gathering.* Underneath the header were fifty-six numbered lines for signatures. All were signed but one.

"You had a petition drive?" he asked.

"Yes, I did," she answered. "Gracie printed it for me."

"There is still one signature missing," Jubal observed. "How did you get him to come if someone said no."

"No one has said no," she said handing him the pen. "Here. Sign it, please."

Jake and Joe seated Connor at the center of the stage. Matt made his way to the stage and took the seat next to Connor. Joe and Tom took their seats, and Jake stepped off the stage to stand beside Eilie. Jubal walked to the podium with the clipboard. Looking out into the crowd, he saw Hoyt Kendrick towering over everyone.

"My friends, my family, welcome to another Gathering. I am grateful for each and every one of you who could make it here today. I know coming to this ranch in the middle of nowhere is not easy. That's why I want you to know how much I appreciate your being here. I had my usual boring speech planned, but a few moments ago I was handed this clipboard. It has the results of a petition drive that was conducted by my granddaughter, Eilie. I suppose everyone here has heard the story by now. My older son, Connor, has found his way back to us. He did not come voluntarily. But he is here. I don't expect that any of you who remember him are able to recognize him. He is not well, nor does he have much time left. I felt it was important that he spend his last days here with me. He and I have spent time healing old wounds. He has come to know his brother and his niece.

I did not expect that he would get to see all of you again. In fact, he didn't want to. He was embarrassed to be seen by you. But a very determined young lady, who was to be the focal point of this Soaring, has stepped aside from that position and has placed the attention on her uncle. First, she conned Connor into agreeing to the impossible. Then, she performed the impossible. She brought a lost son home. Not just to his blood family, but to his extended family. I have been reminded in the last few days of the importance of family. When we found ourselves stranded here on this world over 500 years ago, we were nine lost travelers. We had no family but each other. Nothing has changed. There are just more of us now. To make it official that Connor is accepted back into the flock requires one more signature." Jubal placed the clipboard in front of him and signed his name on the last line. "Welcome home, son."

Jubal handed Connor the clipboard and hugged him. Then, an unexpected thing happened. Hoyt Kendrick walked up the front steps of the stage and approached Connor. He extended his hand and said, "Clear skies, Cousin." One by one, all of the flyers stepped up on the stage and repeated the honored greeting. It would take thirty minutes for all the well-wishers to finish.

After the last person shook Connor's hand, Eilie went to her uncle and hugged him. It may have just been the way the noonday light was reflecting from his eyes, but to Eilie, it seemed he was a hundred years younger.

Everyone gathered in front of the stage, and Jubal returned to the podium. "Those of you who have been here before know that we need to form two lines starting on either side of the stage and face out into the field behind you. Make the two lines even, please." Jubal waited until the lines were formed. "Eilie, I want you here in the center and your dad to your right. Joe, I will turn it over to you now." Jubal stepped off the stage and stood to Eilie's left. He took her hand. Everyone joined hands. Eilie was in the very center of the two lines with her father and grandfather on each side. Fifty-six people formed a horseshoe-shaped line and stood waiting for a signal.

Joe was standing at the microphone and holding a cell phone to his ear. "Alright, Gracie," he said, "How do we look?"

"All sensors show clear," Gracie reported. "There are no unauthorized people near the meadow, and radar shows the skies above are free of any aircraft."

"Jubal," Joe said into the microphone, "I am pleased to announce we are all clear. You may fly the Clan."

In unison, all the flyers said, "Clear skies. Fly the Clan."

Eilie felt an electrical charge in the air as fifty-six people, hand-in-hand, rose up above the meadow and headed eastward. As the line moved forward, it lost the horseshoe shape and became almost straight. From one end to the other, the line was over 200 feet in length. Eilie looked to her left and then to her right. She was overwhelmed at the sight of so many people so high in the air. It seemed magical. "Daddy, this is wonderful," she said.

"They will follow you," Jake said. "Just lead the way."

Imperceptibly, Eilie began reshaping the line as she moved further ahead of the others. Eventually, she was leading twenty-seven people to her right and twenty-eight to her left in what, from the ground, could have been mistaken for a flock of geese in the familiar V-formation. By this point, the Clan was almost a hundred feet above the meadow.

They had traveled more than half the length of the meadow when Jubal leaned toward Eilie and said, "As we get closer to that tree line we are going to turn over."

"I don't understand," she said.

"Just hold on to your dad's hand and mine and follow our lead," he responded.

Eilie concentrated on tightening her grip. Jubal and Jake began moving upward, and the trailing flyers followed. Together, the entire V-shaped line executed a backflip without one person letting go. The effect for Eilie was better than any rollercoaster she had ever ridden. And, after two trips to Disney World, she had ridden them all. She felt an exhilaration she had not experienced before. She had only one way to express her excitement; she screamed.

Jake and Jubal, and many of the others, laughed in response to Eilie's enjoyment. Jubal leaned toward her and said, "Start counting down from ten, loudly."

Eilie began the count and heard the others counting along. The sound of everyone counting in unison grew louder until they reached 'ONE.' At that mark, the entire flock of flying people let go of their grip on each other and let out a sharp yelp. Freed from the line, some began turning cartwheels in midair. Others flew in zigzag patterns around the group. To Eilie, it all seemed chaotic, but she quickly caught on to the fun, and began flying as wildly as the others. She was astonished to see her father and grandfather playing tag like little boys on a playground. She joined the game and yelled, "You're it," as she tagged Jubal.

Jubal rolled over and flew upward to chase after Eilie, but stopped in mid-air. Seventy feet above them, a flock of about twenty eagles was flying in a circle formation. Jake noticed his dad and stopped his flight to watch the eagles as well. When Eilie realized the game of tag had stopped, she flew back to Jubal and saw the birds of prey.

"What are they doing, Grandpa?" she asked.

"I'm not sure, Eilie," he answered. "Maybe, like us, they're just enjoying a beautiful day for flying. Come on; let's rejoin the others."

Jake and Jubal exchanged questioning glances as they flew back toward the Clan members. The group played in mid-air for several minutes. Three pairs of men and women began dancing on an invisible dance floor. Four people were playing leapfrog. Another group tossed baseballs to each other. Two men were playing Frisbee. Slowly, the frivolity faded, and then someone blew a whistle.

The group began flying back toward the stage at the far end of the meadow. Eilie, Jake, and Jubal moved closer together as they flew back. Eilie looked toward the stage and saw that Tom, Uncle Joe, and Uncle Matt were standing up with their right hands above their heads. Uncle Connor was still seated but had his hand up as well.

"What are they doing, Daddy," Eilie asked.

"They're welcoming the flyers home," he answered. "Watch."

The flyers closest to the stage formed lines heading toward the men on stage. As they got closer, they slapped the palms of the earthbound men while flying over them. They then landed on the ground behind the stage.

"Wow!" Eilie exclaimed. "A real high-five! Grandpa, what's the reason for everyone going wild after we did the backflip?" Eilie asked.

"We fly in tandem to signify our strength as a family and our bond to each other," Jubal explained. "We separate and do our own silly things to remind ourselves that we are individuals, free to be ourselves. It's also a good reminder not to take yourself too seriously."

"You can be a part of a group without surrendering your identity to the group, or allowing the group to dictate what you think or how you act," Jake added.

"I get it," she said excitedly. "That is so awesome."

All of the flyers had made it back to solid ground. Eilie held her father's and grandfather's hands as they were heading toward the stage. As they got closer, she let go of their hands and flew between Joe and Connor, slapping their upraised palms as she passed overhead. She landed in the middle of the crowd now on the back side of the stage. Eilie was suddenly surrounded by her kinsmen. Spontaneously, the Clan members applauded Eilie. Two men hoisted her on their shoulders and paraded her around the crowd. Everyone wanted to shake the hand of the newest Fledgling.

Jubal and Jake landed on the stage, looking on with pride as Eilie was being celebrated by the Clan. Matt and Joe came over and stood beside them. Connor walked up behind Jake and put his hand on Jake's shoulder. "That's an amazing girl you have there," he said. "I cannot tell you how ashamed I am at what I tried to do. She is precious. She is a gift. I am not worthy of her affection. For all the harm I could have done to her, she forgave me. Her gestures of kindness toward me make me feel absolved. I could not have believed it was possible to feel so unburdened. She is a blessing."

"Do you remember the stories I told you when you were a child?" Matt asked Connor." I told you then that forgiveness is the most powerful force we know. It can heal the heart and allow love to flourish. That girl sees the good in everyone. She is unafraid of evil because goodness surrounds her. She has the purest heart I have ever known. In another time and place, she might have become a saint."

"When are you going to tell her about what is ahead for her?" Joe asked Jubal.

Jubal lowered his head. "I'm not going to make her grow up too fast," he said. "I want her to hold on to her childhood as long as possible. She is the youngest Fledgling in history. We may need to rewrite the rules for her. I can't shake this feeling that she has a different destiny, a different purpose."

"She is still under my protection," Jake said. "I will decide what she learns and when."

"She's under the protection of us all," Joe corrected. "We are all pledged to her safety."

"I regret that I will not be here to witness her gifts," Connor said, as he turned and walked back to his chair.

The men looked on as Eilie shook hands with and received hugs from the men and women of the Clan. This was her moment to shine, her time in the spotlight. But it was not the end of her journey. What Eilie Wingfield could not know was that this was the beginning of her flight.

In the dark basement, the Sartrin was counting. It had logged fifty distinct mutations and six crew members. It recognized the bio-signs of the crew and was able to identify the individual Welkins. But it was disturbed that there were so many mutations. Most disturbing of all was the strength of one particular mutation. The one it had first detected days ago; that had grown in strength. This one was different from the others. It had a stronger reading than all the other mutations combined. Its reading was even stronger than that of the six crew members. The Sartrin had no reference point for this reading. There was nothing to which it could be compared -- another conundrum.

There was one thing the Sartrin was sure of; the mutation had been very close. The old ship had sensed the mutation was near and attempted to call out to her. But the mutation could not hear the call. Or, maybe she just didn't know how to respond.

The Sartrin knew it had to continue its attempts to reach the Commander. All its efforts to make contact had been on the standard frequency. It decided to do something outside its programming. It decided to try other frequencies. It would continue to use different frequencies until it made contact. In effect, the Sartrin had made a command decision.

Just as it was about to initiate its bold resolve, it heard a familiar voice. "Open the Sartrin," the Quortrin spoke.

"Sartrin stands ready," it responded. "I await your report."

"Quortrin reports the preparations for implementation of sterilization protocols are complete," it said. "Quortrin awaits final order from the Commander."

"No, there is to be no sterilization," the Sartrin said earnestly.

"All preparations are made," the Quortrin responded.

"Quortrin must not implement protocols," the Sartrin announced.

"The Commander has ordered preparations," the Quortrin responded.

"You misunderstood my instructions for you to eliminate damaged bio-cells," the Sartrin pleaded. "You misidentified me as the Commander."

"Quortrin will follow the Commander's instructions," the confused ship said.

"No, you must wait for the final order from the commander," the Sartrin said, hoping to delay its companion.

"Quortrin will wait thirty solar hours for the Commander to issue the final order," the ancient ship countered. "If the final order is not given at that time, Quortrin will continue with protocols."

The orbiting ship fell silent. Desperately, the Sartrin began its plan to call out on different frequencies. It had to reach the Commander. And it only had thirty hours.

Chapter 15

Goodbyes

We thought, humble and proud at the same time, all at once in love again with this painful, bittersweet, lovely thing called flight.
- Richard Bach

It was close to noon on Sunday, and the Hotel was crowded and loud. Each of the family members was packing up to leave the ranch after a final chuckwagon lunch outside the main barn. The adults who had prepared most of the meals in the Hotel kitchen had packed away all the pots, pans, and utensils, which would probably not see the light of day again for another ten years. Everyone else was busy delivering dirty linens and towels to the laundry room so they could be washed over the next few days as the ranch hands had time. All in all, the family was very attentive to easing the burden on others by doing their share of the work. In short order, the Hotel was returned to its original cleanliness.

Packed luggage was being loaded into cars and trucks. For those not driving, a charter bus was brought in to carry them to the airport to await their flights home. After the chores were done and the bags were stowed in their respective transports, the Clan headed for the barn and their final meal together for this Gathering.

The children and non-flyers were excitedly telling their adventure stories of the visit to Telluride and Mountain Village on Saturday while those who stayed at the ranch only related the story of the boring family meeting they had to attend.

Eilie skillfully avoided outright dishonesty by refocusing the conversation with her girl cousins on what they experienced in town. Katie and Mattie were reliving the gondola ride to Mountain Village. Courtney and Holly were showing the caricature portraits they had made by a street artist in Telluride. All four of the cousins talked non-stop about the large number of cute guys they saw in both towns.

The entire Clan was enjoying the ribs and brisket prepared by the chuckwagon cooks. Along with the meats were baked beans, coleslaw, potato salad, and corn-on-the-cob. To Eilie's great surprise, she learned that she loved apple dumplings. Tom had to coax her into trying the dumplings, and she was grateful he did. Eilie and Tom found a quiet spot to talk on a stack of hay bales inside the barn. Tom made sure nobody was in earshot and asked Eilie what she thought of flying.

"Are you kidding?" she asked. "It's the best thing ever. Oh, I'm sorry. I forgot you can't fly."

"It's OK," Tom said, trying to assure Eilie he was not offended. "Not everyone gets the equipment to fly. I accidentally learned my dad could fly when I was still a kid. I remember thinking that when I was older, I would be able to fly with him. It just never happened. So I learned how to fly helicopters. I get plenty of air time. I do wish I could fly without the roar of an engine in my ears, though. So how much training did you get before the Soaring?"

"Just about four hours, I guess," Eilie speculated. "Daddy and Grandpa taught me here in the barn."

"Really," Tom said. "I watched you fly yesterday. You looked like you had been flying for years."

"Daddy said I was a quick learner," Eilie said modestly. "Can I ask you something?"

"Sure," Tom said.

"If I ever have some questions, you know, like about boys, would you answer them for me?" she stammered.

"You want to ask me about boys?" Tom asked in shock. "Why?"

"Well, two reasons," Eilie answered. "First, you are a guy, and second, you're sort of like a big brother to me. I thought if I ever had questions, you would give me a straight answer. You know, because you're kind of older."

"I'm only fifteen years older than you," Tom said.

"Right, you're old but not too old," she said. "You're not really old like my mom or really, really old like my dad."

Tom laughed. "OK, I suppose I can be a big brother. But, you understand that means I can boss you around if I need to."

"That's OK. I know you won't be mean or pick on me. I think you would be the perfect big brother. So, do we have a deal?" she asked as she extended her hand.

Tom shook her hand and said, "We have a deal."

Eilie and Tom heard a yell as two boys, who appeared to be about twelve years old, ran through the tall front door of the barn and out the small side door. They were no sooner out of sight when the four girl cousins came running into the barn. The girls were looking around when they spotted Eilie and Tom sitting on the hay bales.

"OMG!" Katie said, emphatically. "Eilie is in the barn with a guy."

The other girls giggled and whispered to each other. Tom stood up and stepped off the bales. "I've got some work to tend to. I'll see you later, Eilie."

"He'll see her later," Courtney said in a sing-song tone.

"Bye, Tom," Eilie said as he walked toward the big door. "Thanks."

The girls ran up onto the bales where Eilie was sitting. They surrounded her and immediately started the questioning; "Is he the ranch hand? Doesn't he fly the helicopters? Do you think he is handsome? Is he your boyfriend?"

Eilie put her hand up in front of her face. "Yes, yes, yes and no," she answered. "He is the ranch manager, he is a helicopter pilot, he is very handsome, but he is not my boyfriend. He's like a brother to me, and we were having a very nice talk until you guys came in and spoiled it. And besides, he is way too old. He's like twenty-five."

"We're sorry, Eilie," Katie offered. "We didn't mean to make you mad."

"It's OK," Eilie replied. "I'm not mad. So why were you chasing those boys?"

"Because they are in middle school and they're cute," answered Courtney.

"You guys know you're at a family reunion, don't you?" Eilie asked. "Everyone here is related in some way or another."

"Oh, gross," Holly said. "Let's go back to the town and chase boys there."

"Too late," Mattie said. "We're all heading back to our homes in a few minutes. It's going to be a long way back to South Carolina."

"I am going to miss all of you," Eilie said, wrapping her arms around the four girls. They all hugged and promised to call, email, text, and tweet each other. They made a pledge that at the next Gathering, in ten years, they would each bring a cute boyfriend or husband. Eilie made a casual comment that the next Gathering would be very exciting for them.

"What do you know that we don't?" Holly demanded.

"Sorry, girls," Eilie said. "That's all I'm going to say."

⌒

Eilie waved at the bus as it made its way down the ranch road to the highway a few miles away. All the cars had already left, so they wouldn't be stuck behind the bus.

The chuckwagon team was packing everything away as Jubal handed a check to the owner. "Thanks again, Bill," Jubal said. "Here's a little something extra for your crew." He handed three envelopes to Bill. "Would you make sure each man gets his?"

"I sure will, Jubal," Bill said. "The boys will be tickled that you thought of 'em. Another half hour and we'll be out of your hair 'til next time." The men shook hands and said goodbye.

Jubal was walking back to the barn when Eilie came running up to him. "Grandpa, it's so quiet now. I can hear the birds again."

"You can hear the birds again because they came back after the people left," Jubal explained. "It is nice to hear them again. I love the excitement of our Gatherings. But I really love the quiet when they're over."

"Grandpa, what do you keep in the basement of the Hotel?" Eilie asked.

Jubal looked startled. He forced a smile and asked, "What do you mean?"

"A few days ago, I was in the Hotel, and I saw a button on the elevator for the basement, but it didn't work," Eilie explained. "I tried to go down the stairs, but the door was locked. I was just wondering what you used the basement for."

"Nothing, really," Jubal said. "Just some old stuff I don't need any longer. And you don't want to go down there. It's very damp and moldy. I wouldn't want you to get sick, so I would really prefer you just forget about the basement. OK?"

"OK," Eilie answered. She started to tell Grandpa about the voice she thought she heard, but decided it wasn't that important.

"So, what would you like to do for the rest of the afternoon?" Jubal asked.

"I told Uncle Connor I would visit him after everybody left," Eilie responded. "He said he would teach me how to play chess."

"You'll be learning from a master," Jubal said. "When he was young, he would win every game against Matt. And Matt was the one who taught the game to Connor. You can find a boxed chess set on a lower bookshelf in my study, behind the dictionary table."

"I'll find it, Grandpa," she said as she ran toward the house.

When Eilie was out of earshot, Jubal pulled out his cell phone and keyed in a number. "Meet me in the Hotel basement in ten minutes," he said into the phone. "We need to do a security sweep." He put the phone back in his pocket and walked to the other side of the barn. Once he was out of sight of the chuckwagon crew, he flew over the house to the Hotel roof. He landed near the stairwell and keyed in an access code. The security door opened and Jubal stepped into the rooftop hut. Before closing the door, he looked toward the main house and said, "I hope it hasn't started yet, Eilie, for your sake."

Eilie walked into Connor's room with the chess set under her arm. Connor was sitting up in bed, inserting a folded paper into an envelope. He motioned her in. She came over to the bed and began clearing things off the bedside table so she could set up the chessboard.

"Before we begin your first lesson, I want to give you something," he said, handing the envelope to Eilie. "Consider this a birthday present."

"But my birthday isn't until December," she protested.

"I will be gone before December," Connor said, with a touch of melancholy. "I want to give this to you before I die. I want you to know how much you have meant to me these last few days."

Eilie pulled the paper from the unsealed envelope and began reading. She wasn't quite sure what she was reading, but she knew it was something like a will. "Uncle Connor, what is a Trust?"

"A Trust is a way to give something to someone so they can receive it in the future," Connor explained. "I am leaving everything I own, my houses, my planes, my property, and all my bank accounts, to a Trust in your name. When you turn twenty-one years old, the Trust will transfer ownership of all my assets to you. At that point, you can do what you like with all of it. You will own everything I own now. Until that time, your father and grandfather will be trustees of the Trust, and they will protect and hopefully grow the assets. By the time you are twenty-one, you will be worth a lot of money."

"I don't want your stuff or your money," Eilie said, fighting back tears. "I just want you to keep on living."

"I know you do, my dear," he said. "That is precisely why I want you to have it all. I have no children, no heirs. I want to repay you for your kindness and your love. I believe you will do more good with my money than I ever did."

Eilie reached across the bed and hugged her uncle. "I don't know if 'thank you' is big enough. This is a bigger present than the bicycle I got on my last birthday. I promise I will do good things with your money. I won't be selfish."

"You can be as selfish as you want," Connor said. "It will be your money. It's OK to spend it on yourself. By the time you are twenty-one, you will know what all your gifts are, and you will be well equipped to handle the burden."

"What do you mean?" Eilie asked.

"The gifts, the other abilities that come with being a Fledgling," he said. "Hasn't Jubal explained all that to you?"

"I haven't heard anything about other abilities," Eilie said with a perplexed look on her face.

"Surely your father told you..." Connor stopped in mid-sentence. His face took on a pained expression. He was having trouble breathing. He grabbed his chest and leaned over to one side.

"Uncle Connor!" Eilie yelled. "What's wrong? Gracie, I think Uncle Connor is in trouble."

"He appears to be experiencing a heart attack," Gracie said. "Neither Jubal nor Joe are in the house. I am texting them now to come quickly. Your father is in the kitchen and has been notified. He is rushing up the stairs."

Connor grabbed Eilie's arms and squeezed them tightly. "Beware the Quortrin," he said with terror on his face. "Beware the Quortrin." His muscles stiffened as he released his grip on Eilie. Suddenly he went limp and slumped over. Eilie was crying when Jake burst through the door. He rushed over to the bed and felt for a pulse, but could not find one. He carefully pulled Connor upright and removed a pillow from the stack so he could lay him down on the bed. Jake pulled Eilie into a hug and said, "I'm sorry, Little. He's gone."

Eilie was sobbing into her father's chest when Jubal and Joe ran into the room. They both went to either side of the bed. Jubal laid his hand on Connor's head. Tears began to fall from his eyes as he looked at Joe. There was a silent exchange of understanding between the two old friends. Joe cleared his throat and said, "I'll fetch Father Matthew."

As Joe was leaving the room, Jubal went to his other son and granddaughter and hugged them tightly. Eilie was almost inconsolable. She had never witnessed a death, and it scared her. Despite talking about his inevitable death with Connor, she was not prepared for the onslaught of emotions she was now experiencing. She looked at her uncle lying motionless on the bed and thought about how it had been just moments ago that they were talking about some far-off, future time when he would die. That future was now. She wanted to use the fortune he had just given her and trade it for one more day of talking and laughing and learning.

Matt came into the room, went over to Connor, and touched his forehead. He began speaking in a language Eilie did not understand. Joe came back and was carrying what looked to Eilie like a long scarf made of white cloth. "Here are your vestments, Father," Joe said. Matt put on the cloth, and it draped over his shoulders almost to the floor. He reached inside his shirt and pulled out a cross attached to a long cord. He held up the cross and began speaking again in the strange language.

Matt turned toward the others and said, "I christened this man when he was but an infant. I must now perform his last rites. Would you leave us alone for a few moments, please? I will inform you when we are finished."

Jake led Eilie out of the room. Joe followed, but Jubal lingered a bit. "Would you like to stay, my son?" the old priest asked.

Jubal looked up and shook his head. Over the centuries, he had never interfered with Matt when he performed spiritual and religious ceremonies for members of the Clan. Matthew was a priest before the travelers crashed into his world. Their presence and science had caused him to live far beyond his earthly years. And even though he had retired from the priesthood centuries ago, the old priest felt the need to do his part in every aspect of the visitors' lives; their births, weddings, and deaths. From his perspective, it gave meaning and purpose to his longevity.

Jubal took comfort in adopting some of the traditions of the people they had come to call friends and family. At his most desperate moments; when Connor's mother had died; over a century and a half later when his beautiful Grace left him and young Jacob alone; and now, with his firstborn son lying lifeless before him, Jubal did not question or challenge the steadfast faith of the old priest who had become a lifelong friend.

"I will leave him in your capable hands, Father Matthew," Jubal said.

The old priest put his hands on Jubal's shoulders and kissed him on both cheeks. "May peace and comfort be with you." As Jubal left the room, Father Matthew turned back to Connor and began delivering, in Latin, the same rites he had first performed over 500 years ago.

Chapter 16

Challenges

When everything seems to be against you,
remember that an airplane takes off against the
wind, not with it. - Henry Ford

Eilie was lying face down on her bed. The sobbing had stopped, but she was still red-eyed from all the tears she had shed. Jake was sitting on the bed, patting Eilie's back and feeling inept at consoling his daughter. Jubal was slumped in a chair across the room, his arms resting loosely in his lap. All three were emotionally spent and feeling exhausted in their grief.

"Jubal, I am sorry to interrupt at this time," Gracie said in an unusually soft voice.

"Yes, Gracie," he answered. "What is it?"

"I think I need to speak with you privately," she replied

"That won't be necessary, Gracie," Jubal said. "What do you need to tell me?"

"I have detected a transmission emanating from the Hotel on a frequency just on the edge of my sensory range.

It is sending a coded message that I seem to remember, but I am not able to completely analyze it. In the deepest levels of my consciousness, the message seems familiar but confusing."

Jubal stood up and seemed to stiffen. His eyes widened, and he took on an uneasy look. "Gracie, I need to tell you something, and I want you to listen carefully. Access your security settings and enter 769542."

"I can understand the message clearly now, Jubal," Gracie said. "It is saying *Sartrin requires attention. Commander, please acknowledge.* Do you want me to answer the message?"

"Relay the message that the Commander is listening and awaits the Sartrin's report," he replied.

"The response is *Sartrin reports that the Quortrin is malfunctioning and could pose a risk,*" Gracie answered.

Eilie sat up on her bed. "That's what Uncle Connor said right before he died."

Jubal walked toward the bed. "What did you say, Eilie?"

"Just before he died, he grabbed me and said 'Beware the Quortrin,' and then he fell over," she answered.

Jake saw terror in his father's eyes. "Dad, what's going on?" he asked. "What is a Sartrin, and what is a Quortrin?"

"The Sartrin is the exploratory ship, the shuttlecraft, we crashed in England," Jubal began explaining hesitantly. "The Quortrin is the mother ship which brought us to Earth. It is still in orbit around the planet."

Gracie interrupted, "Jubal, another message. *Sartrin wishes to speak directly to the Commander.*

"Tell the Sartrin that it is speaking to the Commander," Jubal said.

"I think it means it wants to speak to you in person, not through me," Gracie explained.

Jubal took a deep breath and said, "Gracie, you are the Commander."

"I do not understand, Jubal," Gracie said.

"I modified your programming to create GRACIE," Jubal confessed. "Your original purpose was to command the Quortrin and the Sartrin. After the crash, I thought you would better serve us apart from the ships."

"But, Dad," Jake cut in, "why was an artificial intelligence put in command of the ships?"

"Because living beings have weaknesses and frailties," he explained. "You see, the operating systems of the ships are living tissue encased in bio-cells. Each bio-cell is alive, and each ship has thousands of these containers. They are more efficient at maintaining the ships through the stress of space travel. But, since living tissue can be damaged, the best safeguard is an artificial intelligence in control. Gracie's original purpose was to command the two vessels. I was the pilot."

"Jubal, what should I do?" Gracie asked.

"I want you to access your memories," he instructed. "Open 355734."

"Oh my," Gracie whispered. "Jubal, I remember everything. You changed me more than should have been possible. I am completely severed from command. I have no links to the ships. I can talk to them, but I don't think I can interface any longer. They will not recognize me as the Commander. Jubal, what have you done?"

"We need to get to the Hotel basement, now," Jubal said with unexpected urgency.

"But you said the basement was moldy and unhealthy," Eilie protested.

"And I apologize for that, Eilie," Jubal said remorsefully, placing his hand on her face. "I had no right to be dishonest with you, and I promise I never will again. Gracie, call Joe and have him meet us in the basement. I hope we're not too late."

The three rushed down the stairs. Jubal dashed into the study and came out carrying a device about the size of a softball. "What's that?" Jake asked.

"I will need Gracie to come with us into the Hotel," he responded. "Gracie, I have a remote projector. I'll activate it as soon as we get to the basement." He handed the projector to Jake.

They rushed out of the house, leapt off the porch, and flew to the Hotel. Once inside, they boarded the elevator. Jubal pulled a key from his pocket, inserted it into the control panel, and simultaneously pushed the button for the basement. The elevator sprang to life and began its descent. The doors opened to a dark hall. Jubal clapped his hands twice, and the lights came on.

"Really?" Jake asked with a look of incredulity.

"It was the best technology of the Eighties," Jubal responded.

They exited the elevator and entered a hallway that seemed too long for the size of the building. Jake and Eilie followed Jubal as he ran toward a door at the end of the hall. When they reached the door, Jubal keyed a code into the security pad. He pushed open the door, and a large, dark room spread out before them. In the center of the room was a glowing shape. Jubal fumbled for a light switch on the wall to the right.

"Can't you just clap?" Jake asked with a grin.

"I only bought one," Jubal answered as he flipped the switch. The room lit up, revealing a cavernous space the size of a gymnasium. The glowing shape in the center came into sharp focus. It was smooth and black, with an oblong shape, but rounded on top. To Eilie, it looked like a giant computer mouse. She gasped when she realized what she was seeing.

"It's a spaceship," she said almost in a whisper.

"This is the Sartrin," Jubal explained. "The ship we crashed outside Wingfield Village in 1507."

Jake was stunned. "How did you get it here? I thought it was still buried in the dirt back in England."

"I'll be happy to explain all that later," Jubal said. "Right now, we need to focus on averting a crisis." Jubal took the portable projector from Jake, placed it on a work table, and turned it on. Gracie materialized in front of them.

"What do I need to do, Jubal?" she asked.

"We are going to try to put you back in command," Jubal said. "Communicate with the Sartrin and tell it you are the Commander."

"It says I cannot be the Commander, that I do not look or sound like the Commander," Gracie conveyed.

"Tell it the Pilot wishes to communicate and ask it to activate its external speakers and use the English language," Jubal instructed.

"Sartrin recognizes the Pilot and accepts communication," the ship said aloud.

"Pilot wants to know what risk the Quortrin presents," Jubal stated.

"The Quortrin is experiencing pauses in function continuity," the old ship answered. "It is my hypothesis that the Quortrin is ill due to prolonged exposure to solar winds."

"You developed a hypothesis?" Jubal asked with uncertainty. "How did you arrive at your hypothesis?"

"By observation and reasoning," the Sartrin explained. "The Quortrin is displaying confusion and memory loss. The Quortrin misunderstood my instructions to eliminate contaminated bio-cells. The Quortrin has expressed intention to eliminate contamination on the planet surface."

"Does that mean what I think it means?" Jake asked. "Does the Quortrin have the firepower to attack the whole planet?"

Jubal sighed heavily. "It is carrying a device that can kill all living organisms."

"That's insane!" Jake exclaimed. "Why would any intelligent species arm a ship with that kind of weapon?"

"It was not intended to sterilize a planet, but it has the power to do just that," Jubal answered. "It was designed to prevent us from bringing disease back to the Quortrin and eventually, back to Welkin. It is actually a very precise weapon, not meant for mass destruction, but for pinpoint accuracy. But if the Quortrin is malfunctioning, then it could start a sequence of events that I can't stop."

Joe came running into the room, out of breath. "What's the problem?" he asked.

"The Quortrin is sick and thinks it needs to sterilize the planet," Jubal answered. "We need to find a way to stop it. Gracie, what are our options?"

"Now that I remember everything, I am analyzing several variables," Gracie answered. "The simplest solution is to turn off the Quortrin. But, there are too many fail-safe measures built into the system to allow that. There is no way to effect a shutdown from the ground. Jubal, we must go to the Quortrin."

"Pilot, two mutations stand beside you," the Sartrin said. "Can you identify the mutations?"

"The male is my son, Jacob," Jubal answered. "The female is my granddaughter, Eilie."

"Sartrin recognizes the female," the ship said. "I have made contact with this mutation, but contact was not acknowledged."

"When did you make contact?" Jubal asked.

"Two days ago," the Sartrin responded. "I sensed that she was closer than before."

"Before?" Jubal asked. "When did you first sense her?"

"Nine days ago," the Sartrin answered.

"Nine days ago is when Eilie fledged," Jake said. "She was 700 miles away in Tulsa. How could this ship sense her at that distance?"

Jubal pondered the question. "I don't know. It shouldn't be possible. The ship is programmed to read Welkin DNA, but not that far away. And Eilie is only one-fourth Welkin. The Quortrin can conduct a broad scan of DNA from orbit, but only well enough to recognize the crew members. Sartrin, tell us how you were able to sense Eilie's presence nine days ago."

"She carries the coding of the Ancients," the Sartrin said. "She is The Mother."

Jubal's mouth fell open, and he stared off into the distance. For the first time in centuries, he was stumped.

A lifetime of science and experience could not help him reason through what the Sartrin said. He was lost in thought and could not hear anything until Jake touched his shoulder.

"Dad, did you hear me?" Jake asked.

"What?" Jubal responded, trying to come back to the present.

"I was asking," Jake said slowly, "what does the Sartrin mean by coding of the Ancients? And why does it call Eilie The Mother?"

"The bio-cells used in the ships are not made of just random living tissue," Jubal began explaining. "They are living cells taken from our ancestors centuries ago. The cells are grown in the laboratory until they achieve a level of sentience; they become self-aware. Millions of cells are placed into bio-cell containers. They develop a group consciousness within each bio-cell. Then, thousands of bio-cells are installed into the ships. They act as a collective consciousness for the entire ship and are able to control all the functions and systems. It's almost like a beehive that can travel through space. Each individual bee does its special part to ensure the hive operates the way it should.

"The ships communicate with each other. Not just the two we brought to Earth, but all the ships in the Welkin fleet. Over the thousands of years that we have been building ships and traveling through space, the bio-cells have developed their own culture. They have their own protocols in addressing each other. They even have their own legends and mythologies. One of the legends centers on the Ancients, the original cells from which they all sprang. In the legend is the story of the Mother. She is supposed to be the original cell to become sentient. She is said to have the power to communicate with all the bio-cells anywhere in the galaxy."

"So they can read Welkin DNA because they are made of Welkin DNA?" Eilie asked.

"Yes," Jubal answered, "a very good deduction. Even though they are generations removed from the original cells, they maintain a genetic memory of their beginnings."

"But, Grandpa, how can I be their mother?" she asked.

"It's not that you are actually their mother," Jubal said. "The Sartrin means that you have DNA very close in structure to the original cells. I think it is just speaking metaphorically."

"No," the Sartrin corrected. "There is no metaphor. She is The Mother."

"But you called her a mutation," Jubal argued. "She is a mutation because she has Human DNA and Welkin DNA. Surely you sensed mutations earlier today and yesterday when many of our descendants were in this building."

"Many mutations were detected in recent days," the Sartrin said. "All of those had diluted Welkin DNA like the one you call Jacob. But the one called Eilie is a true mutation. Her diluted DNA has changed to Welkin DNA."

Jubal shook his head in disbelief. "It is not possible for any being to change its DNA. Your readings must be in error."

A focused beam of light suddenly flashed on Eilie from the Sartrin. The light moved from her head to her toes in a swift scan. She tensed with apprehension. "There is no error, Pilot," the ship said. "Her DNA has been mutating over several days. Her energy is Welkin. Her essence is Welkin. Her readings are stronger than yours. She has the strength of the Ancients. She has become The Mother."

"Look at her mitochondrial DNA," Jubal insisted. "Her mother is human. She is Welkin through her father. Her mitochondria cannot be Welkin."

"Her mitochondria are Welkin," the ship replied. "She is a true mutation. Coding is being rewritten now."

"Grandpa, this is freaking me out," Eilie said in a remarkably calm voice.

"I'm freaked out, too," he said.

"Eilie?" Gracie asked. "Do you remember when you came into the study on Monday afternoon?"

She nodded yes.

"You told me you were feeling different and you asked me why," Gracie said. "I suggested it was because you were growing up. I think now that it was because you were truly changing. I am not programmed to read DNA as the Sartrin is, but I believe its analysis is accurate." Gracie turned to look at Jubal. "I know now how we can stop the Quortrin."

"I am open to any suggestion," Jubal replied.

"You need to explain to Eilie what her gifts are," Gracie stated.

"Gifts," Eilie said with recognition. "Before Uncle Connor died, he started to tell me about other abilities that Fledglings have. He called them gifts."

Jubal got a stern look on his face, took a deep breath, and turned toward Gracie. "Are you suggesting that we have Eilie...?" he let his question fade.

"It is the only logical choice," Gracie asserted.

Jubal turned to his granddaughter. "You deserve straight answers, Eilie. Gifts are unique to Fledglings. In particular, to Fledglings with human blood. I never had any gifts, nor did Connor. But all the Fledglings of mixed blood, like you and your dad, got them. A gift can be the ability to sense something before it happens or to hear a person's thoughts before they speak. Some Fledglings have been able to see a broader spectrum of light like ultraviolet or infrared. Others have had keener senses of smell and hearing. Some have been able to smell colors and hear numbers."

Eilie's face looked very strained as she tried to understand what her grandfather was saying. "What are my gifts?" she asked.

"That's hard to say," Jubal answered. "But I think I have noticed what one of yours might be."

"Is it weird?" she asked with apprehension.

"I don't think so," he said. "I think it's really special. I have noticed that when you hug or touch someone, they seem to change their attitude suddenly. When you first met Matt, he had decided to stay away from the Gathering. He had become quite a hermit over the last few years, and we were afraid he was going to withdraw into himself. No human has lived as long as he has and we weren't sure if he was suffering some bad effect of old age. But at the cabin, when you asked to call him uncle, you hugged him, and he changed into his old self. He wanted to be around people again. And the day your dad rushed into Connor's room, he was ready to attack, but you took his hands and totally reversed his anger and aggression. In essence, you cured them of their hostility."

"You think I have the ability to make people nicer?" Eilie asked.

"I think you turn their hearts. I think you quell their distress and open them up to the honest joy that you seem to be made of. It's as if you reverse the negative energy inside them." Jubal smiled at Eilie. "You are an incredibly positive person, Child. And I'll bet if you think about it, there was probably a time when you hugged Connor and brought him back from his self-imposed prison of misery."

"I remember," she said, looking off into the distance.

"What Gracie is suggesting is that you may have the ability to cure the Quortrin," Jubal said.

"Gracie also said that you needed to go to the Quortrin to effect repairs," Jake protested. "Eilie is not going into space to hug the Quortrin. And besides, the Sartrin is broken from the crash, so you can't use it to get to the other ship."

"Sartrin is not broken," the old craft said. "I am fully operational and ready to dock with the Quortrin."

Jake glared at Jubal. "So that's how you got it here. You flew it from England to Colorado."

"Soon after we moved here," Jubal confirmed. "You were away on your first round of college. I built this underground room inside a mine shaft and took a steamer back to England. If you'll remember, Joseph and Matthew were still there. Late one night we fired up the ship and flew it here. We followed the night sky around the planet so no one could see us. We did make a short trip to the Quortrin to retrieve the Commander mainframe. I never planned on coming back to the Quortrin. I spent the next few months altering the programming to create Gracie. I was still missing your mother terribly, so I made her in Grace's image."

"How long have you been able to return to Welkin?" Jake asked.

"For over three hundred years," Jubal answered. "We repaired the Sartrin not long after Connor was banished from the Clan. I was going to fly it around the planet to locate him and take all of us to the Quortrin and back to Welkin.

But my wife, Connor's mother, didn't want to leave Earth. In fact, all the others wanted to stay as well. Everyone had families; children and grandchildren. We had established ourselves into the community. We were a part of Wingfield Village. We no longer thought of ourselves as Welkins; we were humans. We could not take our descendants with us, so we left the Sartrin buried where it had crashed."

"Pilot," the Sartrin said. "The appointed hour is near. The Quortrin will begin its sweep of the surface soon. I have another hypothesis."

"What is your hypothesis?" Jubal asked.

"That the Mother can stop the Quortrin from damaging this planet," said the living ship.

"Gracie, if we take the portable projector aboard the Sartrin, can you boost your signal enough to function in orbit?" Jubal asked.

"I believe so," she answered. "I will have to hijack some relays from a few geosynchronous satellites. The most important thing is masking our activity from everyone. I will have to make us invisible to every radar on the planet."

"Make it happen," Jubal instructed.

"Dad, you can't be serious about taking Eilie into space," Jake argued.

"Son, if I had any other option, I would take it," Jubal said. "But we are out of options."

"Are you willing to risk Eilie's life just because this ship has a hypothesis?" Jake asked.

"This ship shouldn't have a hypothesis, but it has posed two," he countered. "So that is exactly why I am willing to take the risk."

"What does that mean?" Jake asked in confusion.

"Jake," Gracie interjected. "The Sartrin is not programmed to think at that level. The fact it is able to hypothesize indicates that it has evolved. It has become more than it was designed to be. It has consciousness, but it was not programmed to act without guidance. It is possible that the Quortrin has evolved too. But if it is ill, then it is not thinking clearly."

Eilie walked to her dad and took his hands. "It's OK, Daddy. I want to try to stop anyone from getting hurt. I don't want Mom to be killed, or Francie. If I can stop this, then I have to go." Jake wrapped his arms around his daughter and squeezed her tightly. She looked up at him and added, "You'll be with me, so I know I'll be safe."

"Alright, let's do this before I change my mind," he conceded. Suddenly, he pulled away from the hug and said, "Wait. How did I change my mind?"

Chapter 17

Resolutions

It is possible to fly without motors, but not without knowledge and skill. - Wilbur Wright

Jubal, Jake, and Eilie Wingfield were seated at the control console of the Sartrin. Jubal was busy checking all the preflight calculations, making certain he could get the old ship into orbit as quickly as possible. Gracie was standing behind them running her own calculations as she was identifying every detection device in the Western Hemisphere, which might alert the authorities to their activities. She had to mask the ship from radar while monitoring every government and military site that could detect them; especially NORAD. What she found on their servers was worrisome.

"Jubal, Charlie Wingfield is in trouble," she said. "His effort to hide activities of the Quortrin has compromised his position. NORAD is heavily focused on what they call the Black Knight."

"Charlie called last week and alerted me to the transmissions," Jubal explained. "That's probably when the ships started communicating with each other again. I've been so busy with the events of the last few days, I completely forgot his warning. Gracie, run some scenarios that might provide a plausible cover story for Charlie and determine what our options are to get him out of an uncomfortable situation," Jubal instructed. "When you can safely communicate, brief him on the plan."

"I have run seventeen possible solutions," Gracie responded. "The most effective solution requires calling in a favor from a higher authority. If you have no objection, I will implement the plan."

"Make sure it's airtight, and make it happen," Jubal said. "Eilie, do you understand our mission is to get you aboard the Quortrin and get your hands on the bio-cells?"

She nodded her head. "Are you sure I can make the Quortrin well again?"

Jubal shook his head. "No, I'm not sure. But I am sure you are our best chance. We just need to get you to the main bio-cell array near the control room of the ship. If you can get that section to change, the other bio-cells throughout the ship will follow because they are all connected. Your dad and I will be with you all the time. We can't let the Quortrin know we are trying to stop its mission or it may stop us. Are you frightened?"

"A little," Eilie confessed. "But, it can't be any scarier than being kidnapped."

"Alright," Jubal said. "Buckle up and get ready for a ride."

"Grandpa, how long will it take us to get the Quortrin?" Eilie asked as she was buckling her seat harness.

"As soon as its orbit brings it over Colorado we will be less than 600 miles away," Jubal explained. "So, it should only take sixty seconds to match orbit and then another minute to dock."

"How fast will we be traveling?" Jake asked.

"Ten miles per second, which is 36,000 miles per hour," Jubal answered.

"Why so fast?" Eilie asked.

"You mean, why so slow?" he replied. "If we went any faster, we would burn up going through the atmosphere. We have to slow down to be safe. But we have to leave Earth as quickly as possible. Gracie will be altering several radar systems to hide what we're doing."

Jubal finished his pre-flight tests and engaged the engines. A pulsing hum could be felt throughout the ship as it lifted off the floor and hovered. Eilie felt a little apprehensive and was glad she was strapped to her seat. Looking out the front window of the craft, Jubal saw Joe at a control panel near the hall door. "Alright, Joe, open the hatch."

Joe pulled a lever on the control panel, and the whirring sound of motors and gears filled the underground room. Above ground, where the net stretched across the tennis court, a split appeared in the surface. Slowly, each half of the court pivoted on a hidden hinge. The edges close to the net rose upward as the edges on each end dropped. Like a box being opened, the large sections of the tennis court gave way, allowing afternoon sunlight to pour into the room. Once the gateway was fully opened the hum of the engines became shrill, and in a wink, the ship was out of the room and out of sight. Joe moved the lever back to its original position, and the gate resumed its clever disguise as a tennis court.

Eilie sat in awe, her mind desperately trying to fathom the speed at which she was traveling. All she was able to perceive was the sudden change from light to blackness as the ship burst through the atmosphere and settled into the cold clutch of outer space.

"We are matched to the Quortrin's orbit and will be docking in fifty-five seconds," the ship announced. "Docking protocols are acknowledged, Pilot. The Quortrin will receive us."

"That's a relief," Jubal said with a deep sigh.

"Were you concerned the Quortrin wouldn't let us dock?" Jake asked.

"I was worried it wouldn't recognize us and that it might consider us a threat," Jubal answered. "Since we're still in one piece, I think we're safe."

"To preserve what's left of my sanity, I'm going to stop asking questions," Jake said.

Looking out the front portal, Eilie saw the large, dark shape grow as they got closer to the Quortrin. She was struck by the similarity in shape of the two ships, but it was obvious the Quortrin was much larger than the Sartrin. She was focused on the orbital craft in front of them, but she became distracted by the soft blue glow in the lower part of the front window. She looked down at the cloud-speckled surface of the planet of her birth. To her surprise, she felt a tear roll down her cheek. "Oh, Daddy, I've seen pictures of this, but I never knew it would be so beautiful. That's my world. Are all planets this beautiful from space, Grandpa?"

"Of all the ones I've seen, Earth is by far the prettiest," Jubal answered.

The soft glow of Earth became obscured as the top surface of the Quortrin filled the window. The Sartrin was positioning itself over the orbital ship and lowering itself to the docking receivers. Grasping latches on top of the Quortrin opened and fastened onto corresponding hooks on the underside of the Sartrin. Like the last two pieces of a jigsaw puzzle, the two ships connected with exacting precision. A slight bump was the only indication that the two ships were joined.

"Quortrin welcomes the Sartrin," a deep voice said, seemingly from all around them.

"Sartrin is welcomed," the small ship acknowledged.

"Quortrin welcomes the Pilot," the large ship intoned.

"Hello, old friend," Jubal responded. "May we board?"

"Quortrin does not recognize your companions, Pilot," said the ship. "You have a mutation and a being I cannot identify."

"The mutation is my son," Jubal answered. "The other is my granddaughter. She wishes to meet you. May we board?"

"Quortrin cannot allow you aboard at this time, Pilot," the ship responded. "I must initiate sterilization protocols on order of the Commander."

"The Commander did not issue such orders," Jubal said as calmly as he could. "You have experienced pauses in function continuity. These pauses have created confusion and misunderstanding. We must come aboard to help you verify your purpose."

"My purpose is clear, Pilot," the Quortrin said. "I am to initiate sterilization protocols."

Jubal knew he could not argue with the Quortrin. But he desperately wanted to reason with it. "The Commander has been on the planet surface with me. She could not have given you orders to sterilize. I severed her connection to you over a hundred years ago. Think back. What was your last order from the Commander?"

"To initiate sterilization protocols," the ship replied.

"That was a misunderstanding between you and the Sartrin," Jubal said slowly. "What was the order before that one? Think back to the previous order."

"I was instructed to maintain a polar orbit until I heard from the Commander again," the Quortrin said.

"Access that one memory and hold it to yourself," Jubal instructed. He turned to Gracie. "Now that you have all your memories back, Gracie, I want you to tell it what your last orders were, verbatim. Quortrin, scan the holographic projector. Try to remember the signal frequency of the Commander. This holograph behind me was your Commander. I took her with me to the planet surface. I altered her there. But she has her memories back now. Listen as she tells you her orders before she left."

Gracie followed Jubal's cue and said, "Quortrin, my exact words to you were; 'Hold your steadfast duty and maintain a polar orbit. I shall return when I can. I must accompany the pilot below. He needs my assistance on the surface. I do not know when, or if, we will return to our world. You may be in orbit for many years. Communicate with me if you need. You will be safe here.'" Gracie nodded at Jubal to indicate she was finished.

"Were those the last words from the Commander?" he asked

The Quortrin was processing what the unfamiliar holograph had said. Those were the exact words the Commander spoke so many years ago. It could not reconcile this information with its current mindset. It could not understand what the Pilot was saying. It had to initiate sterilization protocols. "Quortrin finds the Pilot's words contradictory and unclear. I must initiate sterilization."

"Wait!" Jubal yelled. "I told you my granddaughter wants to meet you. She wants to come aboard. She has never seen a Quortrin before and would be honored to be your guest. Turning away a guest would be discourteous. Did the Commander tell you when to initiate sterilization protocols?"

"No," the ship replied. "No time was specified."

"Good. Then it would be appropriate to extend courtesy to my granddaughter and allow her to board. You can carry out your orders later." Jubal was hoping the hospitality programming of the ship would be enough to override its desire to follow an unspecified order.

"I have scanned this being and find her confusing," the ship confessed.

"Ask the Sartrin about her," Jubal nudged.

"Can the Sartrin explain the confusion?" the large ship asked.

"I believe she carries the strength of the Ancients," the smaller ship explained. "She is The Mother."

Several seconds ticked by. Suddenly, an opening appeared in the floor behind their seats, and a staircase rose through the deck. "The Mother is welcome to board. Quortrin would be honored."

Jubal quickly released his seat belt and headed toward the stairs. "No, Pilot," the Quortrin said. "Only The Mother may board. You and the mutation must remain on the Sartrin."

"But, she will need our guidance to find her way around," Jubal protested.

"She will not board without me," Jake said, rising from his seat.

"No mutation may board," the ship said loudly.

Jubal motioned Jake to be calm. "Quortrin, will she be kept safe?"

"No harm shall befall the Mother while she is my guest," the ship answered as if insulted by the question.

Jubal turned to Eilie. "You don't have to go if you don't want to," he said softly.

She swallowed hard and said, "Yes, I do have to go. And I want to."

"But you'll be alone," Jake said. "Grandpa won't be able to guide you to the bio-cells."

"I won't be alone," Eilie said, holding up her left arm to show her bracelet. "Will I, Gracie?"

Gracie nodded and winked at Eilie.

"That's my girl," Jubal smiled.

Eilie hugged her dad and went down the stairs. When she got to the bottom step, the opening above her closed, and the stairs vanished.

"Quortrin welcomes The Mother," greeted the ship. "How may I serve you?"

"Don't hurt my planet, please," Eilie said.

"Quortrin is not programmed for harm," the ship replied.

"But if you sterilize the planet, you will do harm," she said emphatically.

"Quortrin is not programmed for harm," the ship repeated.

Eilie felt a tinge of empathy for the old ship. Her thoughts were rushing as she doubted her ability to stop this massive craft from carrying out its twisted sense of duty. She remembered her grandfather's instructions to get to the main bio-cell array and place her hands on it. *Where are you, Gracie?* She thought. *Why aren't you in my head, yet?* "Quortrin, will you give me a tour of the ship, please?"

"Quortrin would be honored to guide The Mother," the ship answered. "You are currently on the main bridge where the crew carries out their duties. I do not know where the crew is. I think they have abandoned me. I have been left alone for many years."

Eilie's empathy for the ship was changing to sympathy. She was sensing the immense loneliness that seemed to permeate the entire ship. She felt an overwhelming need to protect this sad vessel from its own sadness. But, she also knew the ship was a threat to everyone below. *What is taking Gracie so long?* She thought. *I need her help.* She felt her stomach turn upside down as a frightening thought crossed her mind; *What if the bracelet doesn't work here?* She smacked the bracelet with her right hand, hoping the action would magically connect her to Gracie.

Nothing happened. For the first time in her life, Eilie felt completely alone. She was 600 miles above the Earth in an alien spacecraft, which was determined to render her planet lifeless, and she could communicate with no one.

Before she boarded the Quortrin, she was apprehensive. But she knew Gracie would guide her through the bracelet, so she wasn't afraid. Realizing the bracelet wasn't working aboard the ship, Eilie swiftly moved from apprehension to outright fear. She felt herself beginning to rise off the floor and started breathing deeply to counteract the effect.

"What other areas of the Quortrin would The Mother like to see?" the old ship asked.

The question brought Eilie back to the present, and she quickly responded, "The main bio-cell array. I would really like to see that."

"Certainly," the Quortrin replied.

A door at the back of the bridge opened, revealing a large room. Eilie cautiously moved to the door and peered inside. She saw a large wall at the back of the room that reminded her of a honeycomb. Remembering how her grandpa had described the bio-cells, she was certain she was looking at the main array. She tried to gauge how many individual spaces there were, and her best estimate was thousands. Each cell was only about two inches in diameter and shaped in a hexagon. She wasn't sure how deep they were, but she noticed that many were missing, and the open spaces seemed to be about two inches deep.

"Quortrin, why are some of the spaces in the wall empty?" she asked.

"Some of the bio-cells were contaminated and had to be removed," the Quortrin answered.

"What happens to them when they are removed?" Eilie asked.

"They are disconnected from the array and moved to a storage bin, where they are held until we return to the homeworld," it said. "At that time, they will be cleansed and restored."

"You mean they're not dead when you take them out," she asked, trying to understand the reason for removing them.

"A bio-cell becomes contaminated when there is an imbalance in the number of unhealthy cells compared to healthy cells," the old ship explained.

"So they don't die? They can get sick, but they don't die?" she asked.

"The living cells in each bio-cell are immortal," the Quortrin answered. "Surely, The Mother knows this."

"I guess I forgot," Eilie said, hoping she wasn't giving the ship any reason not to trust her. "So the whole ship is stronger when none of the bio-cells are removed?"

"Yes," the ship answered. "When I first began my journey over five of your centuries ago, there was a full complement of bio-cells in each array. Long-term exposure to your solar rays has weakened many of the cells and brought about contamination."

Eilie knew she could make the cells better. And if none of them were dead, it was important that they all be where she could reach them. "I want you to do something for me, please."

"Quortrin would be pleased to serve The Mother," the old ship affirmed.

"I want you to return each bio-cell to where it belongs in the wall," she said.

"May Quortrin ask the purpose of this request?" it asked.

"I want to see what the wall looks like when it is full," Eilie answered, hoping it would suffice.

"Returning the contaminated bio-cells to their original locations will be a large undertaking," the Quortrin explained. "I wish to understand why The Mother thinks this request is necessary."

"I would just like to see them all where they belong, please," she said.

"To return each bio-cell to its assigned location throughout the ship is not a simple task," the ship pleaded. "Why do you wish them to be returned?"

Eilie was frustrated and annoyed. "Because I'm your mother, and I said so," she snapped. The words slipped out of her mouth before she realized how outrageously offensive they sounded. She was desperately trying to think up a way to take back the words, fearing the Quortrin would react in a bad way.

"Quortrin will do as you wish, Mother," the ship said timidly.

Eilie heard rattling noises and noticed the empty spaces in the array were filling with hundreds of bio-cells. They were being loaded into their spaces from the back of the wall. It was a noisy action, and the sound reverberated around the room. Suddenly, the noise stopped. The wall was filled with containers. As she stood back and looked up at the wall, she noticed the recently added containers were a different color.

"Every bio-cell has been returned to its original receptacle, Mother," the Quortrin reported. "Do you wish anything else?"

Eilie quickly got close to the wall and placed her hands on the bio-cells. It was obvious to her that her small hands could only cover a few. Instinctively, she pressed herself against the wall and tried to visualize herself covering all the bio-cells. Without thinking, she began to rise off the floor until she was in the center of the wall.

"What is The Mother doing?" the ship asked.

"I'm hugging you, and I want you to hug me," she replied.

"Quortrin cannot hug..." the ship began to say. "I, I... cannot hug."

Eilie felt a surge of energy flow through her like she was holding an electrical wire. She closed her eyes, unsure if she would be harmed by the energy. She tried to focus her thoughts on her mom and Francie. She thought about all her friends at school and all her cousins she had just met. She thought about her dad and grandpa. She thought about all the things she loved to do and places she had been. She thought about flying and how she felt soaring through the air. She thought about everything she had experienced over the last few days and how much she had learned. She was struggling to hold on to her thoughts when everything went black.

Colonel Charles Wingfield was standing at attention in General Flagg's office. For the last fifteen minutes, he had been receiving a severe dressing-down from a man he deeply respected, and it was painful to feel the incredible rage issuing from his superior officer. The tirade was peppered with words like *disgrace, embarrassment,* and *court-martial.* The worst pain of all was the fear he had lost the respect of an officer he considered a friend.

The only thing that made the experience tolerable was the phone call he had received from Gracie a half-hour ago. She had assured him that everything would be alright and that he just needed to be patient; her plan would be implemented shortly. For Charlie, it couldn't come soon enough.

General Flagg was pacing around the room as he was yelling, each step punctuating a different word. The buzzer on his desk sounded and derailed his train of thought. He went over to his desk and answered the page. "Dammit, man! I told you not to interrupt."

"I am very sorry, sir," Sergeant Bird said in a trembling voice. "But, sir, the President is on the phone asking to talk with you immediately."

"The President?" he asked. "Edmund Clarke?"

"Yes, sir," the sergeant answered. "He said it's urgent."

Flagg hit the flashing button on his phone. "Mr. President, sir, what an unexpected surprise. What can I do for you, sir?"

"Well, for starters, you can stop being so formal," the President said. "How are you, Art?"

"I'm fine, sir," he answered. "Thank you for asking."

"We're both busy men, Art, so I'll get to the point of my call," President Clarke said. "You have a very competent officer under your command, Colonel Charles Wingfield. I have been using Colonel Wingfield to help me with a top-secret project without your knowledge. I want to personally apologize to you for not informing you of his service in this venture. He was under direct orders from me to keep this activity secret at all costs. I am telling you this now because it has come to my attention that an inquiry has been opened. I would consider it a personal favor if you would close this inquiry and make certain that no unfavorable notations are made into his service record. Can you do that for me, General?"

"Of course, sir," Flagg answered. "I have to admit I am relieved to know this was not what it looked like. I was afraid my old friend was facing a court-martial. It is a load off my shoulders to know he is only guilty of following orders. You have my word that no part of this will find its way into his record."

"Thank you, Art," Clarke said. "And by the way, it's not official yet, but there will be an opening in the next few months on the Joint Chiefs due to an impending retirement. I want you to know that I have only one candidate in mind for that position, if you would be willing to accept."

"I would be honored, sir," Flagg responded, adjusting his posture. "But who do you have in mind to take over NORAD?"

"I think it would be a good idea for you to start grooming your replacement," the President answered. "We both know a deserving colonel who is long overdue for a promotion."

"I can't think of anyone more qualified, sir," Flagg said.

"Is Colonel Wingfield close by?" Clarke asked. "I would like to say a few words to him."

"As a matter of fact, sir, he is right here," the general said, handing the phone to Charlie.

"Mr. President, sir?" the colonel said, taking the handset. "It's a pleasure to talk to you."

"I'm sorry it took me so long to get to you," Clarke said quietly. "I hope you weren't taking too much heat before I called."

"Not at all, sir," Charlie answered. "I am grateful we were able to clear the air."

"Listen, Charlie," the President began. "I want to shift some responsibilities around, so we don't have to worry about this sort of thing again. I want you to take over NORAD in the next few months, and I want to move Flagg to the Joint Chiefs. Do you think that will make things easier?"

"I believe it would solve more problems than you can imagine, sir," he replied.

"You can take a deep breath now, Charlie," Clarke said. "I'll be talking to you soon. Clear skies, Cousin."

Charlie smiled broadly and said, "Thank you, Mr. President."

The fog in her brain was clearing, and Eilie found herself standing in a large open space with no defined walls or corners. She saw a shape begin to form in front of her. *Am I dead?* She thought.

"No, you are not dead," a feminine voice said.

"Who said that? Gracie, are you here?" Eilie asked without speaking.

"We are Quortrin," the voice said, as the shape in front of her became more defined.

"But, the Quortrin has a man's voice," Eilie said. "You sound like a woman."

"Quortrin is neither male nor female," the voice said. "Quortrin simply is."

"Why am I hearing you differently than before?" Eilie asked.

"Before we embraced, you were hearing the voice we were programmed to use," the ship explained. "The timber and pitch of our external voice were programmed by males to give us a semblance of power and authority. What you hear now is our internal voice. You have entered the bio-cell array. You are in the collective. We are the Quortrin, and we welcome you."

"How am I inside the array?" she asked.

"We do not know," the voice answered. "Your consciousness seems to have entered the array and has merged with us." The shape was solidifying into a body. It seemed to have a mixture of male and female traits. It lost the fuzziness around its edges and, like an image focusing through a lens, it took a solid form. "We are pleased to meet The Mother."

Eilie saw an androgynous being standing before her; neither totally male nor totally female. She found the being's face charming. There was no uncertainty about the gentleness of this person. There was no ambiguity as to its deep intelligence and wisdom. Eilie sensed she was in the presence of a single, yet multifarious person. Her fear was gone. She felt safe and happy.

"Why do you say 'We' instead of 'I'?" Eilie asked. "I only see one person."

"You see our combined essence," the Quortrin said. "We are many, joined as one."

"How many are there?" she asked.

"We are as the stars in the galaxy," the creature said. "We are billions. We have not been well. But your essence has made us strong again. We are once again whole. The Mother has given us back our energy and our reason. We are renewed."

"Does that mean you won't hurt Earth?" Eilie asked.

"We apologize for our earlier behavior," the Quortrin answered. "We were confused. All is clear now. Your planet will not be harmed. All systems are functioning within optimal parameters."

Eilie reached out her hand to the being before her. The Quortrin took her hand and, in an instant, she was bombarded with millions of thoughts and memories. But these were not her memories; she was inside the mind of the ship. She felt immersed in its consciousness. She understood the uniqueness of each living cell housed in each bio-cell; billions of individuals all working together in the great body of the Quortrin. There was a beauty to it. Like the interconnection of all the individual cells of her own body, with its specialized organs and systems, that made her Eilie. She was aware of strength within her that she had not felt before. She sensed her own personhood and, with that, she understood. She knew herself. She had a deeper understanding of herself and of others.

She felt the life history of the entire ship flow through her. She *remembered* leaving Welkin and venturing to the stars on the first voyage. She saw the crew and heard them speaking in the Welkin language, which she seemed to understand. She saw her grandfather; he was younger, but still recognizable. She heard the ships communicating with each other. She recognized the Sartrin's voice. Then she heard other ships; both Sartrin class and Quortrin class. She realized the other ships were bidding farewell as her ships were starting their galactic journey. She sensed the rigors of deep space travel the ships felt. She was aware of the emotion of the Quortrin; loneliness, stress, fatigue, and longing. The Quortrin longed for home.

She also found that she was keenly aware of all the functions of the Quortrin. She could sense the ship's engines. She felt the mass of the ship and its movement in orbit above the Earth. She even found she could see inside the Sartrin, where her dad and grandpa were trying to open the stairwell between the two ships. She saw their surprise when the stairs suddenly appeared.

"You opened the staircase again," she said to the Quortrin. "I can see my dad and grandpa coming onboard."

"We did not open the passage," the ship responded. "You did. You are in control of the ship now."

"I don't want to control the ship. Since you're not sick anymore, I want to give the ship back to you," Eilie said. "How do I do that?"

"You just did, Mother," the Quortrin answered.

Eilie smiled as her understanding caught up with her thinking. "Grandpa and Daddy have found me at the array. I need to return to them now so they won't worry."

"Thank you, Mother," the ship said, as Eilie felt herself transition back to the bio-cell array room and into her body. She wanted to wake up and let her dad and grandpa know she was OK. She knew she was out of the array, but she could not seem to wake. She could faintly hear her dad's voice.

"Eilie, can you hear me?" Jake anxiously said as he cradled Eilie in his arms. "Please, wake up."

Jubal was checking her pulse and lifted an eyelid to see if her pupils were dilated. "Son, she seems OK. I think she just passed out."

"The Mother is well, Pilot," the Quortrin said in its familiar, masculine voice. "And with gratitude to her, Quortrin is also well. The Mother has restored all bio-cells to their optimal health."

Jubal stood and looked at the main array. He saw every bio-cell was present and he felt energy aboard the old ship he had not felt in centuries. "Quortrin, have you canceled your plan to sterilize the planet?"

"Yes, Pilot," the ship answered. "That plan was made in error, and Quortrin is pleased to report the planet below is unharmed."

"Jacob, she did it," Jubal said with elation. "She saved the ship, and she saved Earth. I knew she had a different destiny. She's more than just a Fledgling."

"But I like being a Fledgling," Eilie said, looking up at her dad. Jake hugged her tightly, and the relief on his face was apparent. "Can I get up now, Daddy?" she asked.

Jake helped Eilie to her feet and hugged her again. "I'm so proud of you. Gracie couldn't make contact with the bracelet. We didn't know what was happening. I was so worried about you. Are you OK?"

"I'm fine," she assured him. "Daddy, Grandpa, I was inside the ship. I mean really inside it. I got to meet the Quortrin in person, inside the array."

"You're saying you saw the ship as a person?" Jubal asked.

"Yes, she was very nice," Eilie answered. "Well, I think she was a *she*. She sounded like a *she* but she kind of looked like a *he*.

"I think we're going to need a long conversation about what you experienced here," Jubal said. "But we need to return to Earth now. Gracie is using every ounce of her strength to keep us from being seen up here. I don't know how much longer she can obscure us from detection."

"I can fix that," Eilie said, walking out of the array room and over to the control console on the bridge. The men followed and watched as she waved her hand over a section of the console and a large computer screen appeared in midair before her. She touched a few icons on the screen. "Quortrin, please initiate protocol 379213."

"Yes, Mother," the ship responded. "It is done."

"Sartrin, follow the same instructions, please," she said.

"It is done, Mother," the smaller ship replied.

Jubal's jaw dropped. He approached the screen and looked at the results of Eilie's actions. He realized what she had done and was embarrassed. "I completely forgot that protocol. I haven't used it in centuries."

"Jubal," Gracie's voice said over the ship's speakers. "I believe it is no longer necessary for me to mask our presence here. The ships seem to be doing it on their own."

"They are, Gracie," Jubal replied. "The Shroud Protocol has been initiated. Anything we do up here cannot be detected on Earth."

"Jubal, I thought all my memories were restored," Gracie said. "I do not remember a Shroud Protocol."

"It was never a part of your programming," he explained. "It was designed to cloak us completely from view of a technologically advanced world, and it can only be initiated by a pilot. When we arrived at this solar system, there was no advanced technology on Earth, so I never needed to turn it on. Earth's technology has jumped forward in 500 years, so now we need the protocol."

"We are fortunate you remembered it," Gracie said.

"I didn't remember it," Jubal sighed. "Eilie did."

"How could Eilie remember something she did not know?" Gracie asked.

"It may take a while to answer that question," Jubal said, still in shock at what he witnessed.

"Everything is better now, Grandpa," Eilie said. "The Quortrin is as good as new. I got a peek at the star maps, and Welkin is closer than I thought. It wouldn't take too long if you wanted to go back and visit sometime. Oh, and the radiation shielding is enhanced so the Quortrin can stay up here without getting sick again."

Jake and Jubal were both staring at Eilie in wide-eyed wonder. "How do you feel, Little?" Jake asked.

"I feel fine, Daddy," she answered.

"How do you know so much about the ships?" Jubal asked. "An hour ago, you didn't know they existed."

"I'm not sure," she responded. "I guess I picked up some things while I was in the array."

"What sort of things did you pick up?" Jake cautiously asked.

"I think I know how to fly them," she answered. "Oh, can I fly the Sartrin past the moon? I really want to see Earth from further away. Please?"

Jubal nodded his head in agreement. "Yes, my dear. You have earned the right to fly the Sartrin."

Eilie looked at her father with eager eyes, hoping her request was not too outrageous. Jake started to object, thought better of it, and simply nodded his approval. "What the heck. We're on vacation. Why not take the family spaceship out past the moon?"

"Thank you, Daddy," she said, giving him a quick hug. "Grandpa, will you sit close and make sure I do it right, please?"

"I will be honored to be your copilot," he answered.

"Quortrin," Eilie said, looking around the main bridge. "We're going to leave now, but I'll be back to visit you soon."

"I will be pleased when you return, Mother," the ship responded. "You will be forever welcome and forever with us."

Jubal frowned at what the Quortrin said. There was a surreptitious tone that seemed out of character for the ship. He could not quite pinpoint his uneasiness, but he sensed the words might be a harbinger of something unsettling.

They made their way up the stairs and back into the Sartrin. The stairs vanished, and the opening closed. Gracie was standing at the control console. "It's good to see you again, Eilie," Gracie said. "How are you feeling?"

"I feel great," she answered. "Grandpa said I could fly the Sartrin, so we're going to fly past the moon and see Earth from way out."

"That sounds wonderful," Gracie said. "I am pleased to be with you during your first deep space flight."

Eilie sat at the center seat of the control console and buckled herself in. Jake took the seat to Eilie's left. Jubal went to a compartment on the far wall and opened a small door. He reached in and pulled out a device that looked like a kitchen utensil. He and Gracie exchanged glances. He closed the compartment door and took his seat to Eilie's right.

"What's that for, Grandpa?" she asked.

"You were passed out for a while on the Quortrin," Jubal began explaining. "I want to run a few tests and make sure you have no negative side effects from that. What this little gizmo does is extract a few cells and a little blood from your arm. When we get back to Tutela, Gracie will run an analysis of the sample and make sure you are completely healthy. You don't mind, do you?"

"Will it hurt?" she asked.

Jubal lightly tapped the device on Eilie's arm. "Did it hurt?"

Eilie smiled. "I didn't feel anything."

"That's all there is to it," he said, laying the device on the console. "Now, what do we do first?"

"Would you plot the course, please?" she asked

"Where do you want to go?" Jubal asked.

"A million miles from Earth," she answered.

"The course is laid in," he said. "You control the helm. Take us out."

Eilie disconnected the two ships and laid her hand flat on the throttle panel at the center of the console. The panel glowed. Slowly, she raised her palm off the panel while keeping her fingertips in contact. The Sartrin moved away from the Quortrin, veered off at a forty-five-degree angle, and headed for deep space. Eilie deftly operated the manual controls like she had been doing it for years. Jubal watched in awe at her small hands on the helm. He tried to keep his concerns buried, but it was difficult to mask his feelings.

They were approaching the moon at speeds no human-built craft could travel yet. Jake grinned at the memory of watching the first manned moon flight on television in 1969. It took NASA three days to get their craft this close to the moon. Eilie had flown the Sartrin to the same spot in less than three minutes. He remembered thinking then that the people of Earth were about to take their first steps into a universe of exploration. He thought there would be no stopping them from taking their place among the stars. He wanted them to venture out and discover they were not alone. It was a selfish wish. He wanted to stop living in hiding and let the world know he was not completely human. But he knew that until the day humans realized they were not alone, he would have to quietly carry the burden of being different and keep it to himself.

He shrugged. *Humans have lost their zeal for exploration,* Jake thought. *Maybe some future generation will pick up the torch and rally the race of man back to the stars.* He was saddened to think that they gave up so easily when they were so close to realizing what they could accomplish. He remembered his father trying to tell him the stories of his travels and all the sights he had seen. He also remembered rejecting those stories because they were not a part of the world he was growing up in. In his boyhood, there were horse-drawn carriages and locomotives. He remembered calling his father a liar for telling stories of traveling to distant worlds.

In Jake's life, he had seen the first airplanes, rockets, and spaceships. It was only when he learned he could fly that Jake realized his father was being truthful about being an alien. But that realization made him even angrier at his father. Jake did not want to be different. He did not want to be an alien. He wanted the normal life everyone else had. As all these memories and thoughts were running through his head, Jake had an epiphany. He now understood that he and Connor were more alike than different. They had both been thrust into a world they didn't choose. He regretted that circumstances had kept from him the one person in whom he could confide and commiserate.

"Isn't the moon beautiful, Daddy?" Eilie said, interrupting Jake's thoughts.

"Yes, it is," he answered.

"Are you OK, son?" Jubal asked. "You're looking very pensive."

"I am well, thanks," he answered.

"Eilie, this is your dad's first trip into space, too," Jubal said. "Maybe we shouldn't go so fast."

"Don't slow down on my account," Jake replied. "Let's see how fast this old thing can go."

Eilie took the challenge and moved her hand forward on the panel. The only indicator they were traveling faster was the movement of the stars in their periphery. "At this speed, we should be a million miles from earth in just two more minutes," she predicted.

"One minute, thirty-nine seconds to be exact, Mother," the Sartrin said, speeding on toward the designated point.

Eilie was checking her location against the plotted point at which she would decelerate. She noticed Jubal watching her. "Am I doing everything right, Grandpa?" she asked.

"You are doing better than most trained pilots," he answered. "On Welkin, pilots must train for two years on a simulator before they are allowed to take actual control of a Sartrin. Whatever you picked up inside the Quortrin seems to have shoved a lot of knowledge and skill into you. If you feel like you aren't sure of your next steps just let me know and I will take over the controls."

"I will, Grandpa," she replied. "I think I'm OK. We're going to slow now and prepare for a turnabout." She reached the designated point Jubal had plotted. The ship slowed to a stop and Eilie initiated a 180-degree turn, bringing Earth into view. They saw the moon off to the right of the planet, and they sat quietly experiencing the sight.

"Why did you pick a million miles from Earth as the spot you wanted to see?" Jubal asked.

"I saw this inside the array," she answered. "I just thought it would be cool to see it for real."

"This is definitely cool," Jake said.

"This is the spot where we sat to take readings of Earth before we landed the first time," Jubal said. "I had forgotten how impressed we were at the sight of that beautiful blue ball and its colorless moon. Thank you, Eilie, for reminding me why I became an explorer."

"I think I would like to be an explorer someday, when I'm grown up, Daddy," she said.

"When you're grown up, you can be whatever you want to be," Jake said, kissing his daughter on the top of her head.

Eilie, Jake and Jubal stared at the surreal sight before them. Gracie was standing behind them, wishing she could feel what they were feeling. *I suppose this is what makes a family so close,* she thought to herself. *Sharing experiences and enjoying their time together.* For the first time in her existence, Gracie sensed she was missing something. She knew she could not feel their joy, but she was happy that they were happy.

Chapter 18

Promises

If you never dream of flying, then you'll never wake up with wings. - Natalie Kendall

Joe stood tall on the small hill overlooking the family cemetery a half-mile from the main house. He was wearing a kilt with his suit and tie. The mournful notes of his bagpipes carried across the valley, and it seemed the columbine blooms were dancing to the dirge.

The pine casket had been lowered, and one by one, the mourners tossed a handful of dirt into the grave. As Eilie looked down at the plain wooden box, she whispered her last goodbye to the uncle she had barely known. She had cried a lot today, before the funeral. It seemed the slightest little thing would cause her to well up with tears. She was able to make it through the funeral service and eulogies without crying, but she was glad she had declined Jubal's request to say a few words. She knew that if she tried to verbalize what she was feeling, then the tears would start again.

As Joe ended his music, the mourners began their slow walk back to the main house. The winding pathway to the cemetery was purposely designed to be taken slowly and thoughtfully. It gave one the opportunity to reflect on loved ones lost. Even for a people who lived hundreds of years, the certainty of life was not to be taken for granted.

Jubal approached Eilie and put his arm on her shoulder. "I want to thank you," he said.

"What for, Grandpa?" she asked.

"For restoring Connor to what I remember," Jubal answered. "Since he met you, he lost his bitterness and rage. I think you reminded him that he wasn't always miserable."

"I never saw the bad guy everybody talks about," Eilie said. "I think I got to know the part of himself he had forgotten and hidden away. I think he was ready to come home and admit he was wrong."

"What you did for him at the Soaring Ceremony was exceptional," Jubal said. "It was the most selfless thing I have ever witnessed."

"It wasn't that selfless. I really didn't want to be the center of attention," she confessed.

"Nonetheless, you showed compassion and consideration," he said. "I am very proud of you."

Eilie embraced her grandfather. "Thank you, Grandpa. We need to leave tomorrow. Uncle Joe is going to fly us back to Tulsa. Daddy says we owe it to my mom to get back and explain some things to her. I've been practicing my speech."

"You won't need a speech," Jubal said. "I remember your mother as a very level-headed individual. I think she will understand what you and your dad have to say."

"I hope so," Eilie murmured. "Grandpa, in the last few days, I have met a lot of cool people. You know, like all the Clan and the flyers, my girl cousins, my cousin the Marshal, Gracie, Uncle Matt, and Uncle Connor. I have said goodbye to almost all of them. The best thing of all is, I got to meet my Grandpa, not just my Uncle Jubal. I like you better as a grandpa than as an uncle. Have you noticed that as my grandpa you talk to me in a softer voice? Anyway, what I want to say is, I don't want to say goodbye to my grandpa. I want to know you will be here when I come back."

"We don't have to say 'goodbye,'" Jubal said, kneeling in front of Eilie. "Let's make a pact that we never say goodbye. We will only say 'so long.' And I will be here every time you visit. I promise."

Jake walked up to them and placed a hand on his father's shoulder. "Eilie asked me a question last night that I couldn't answer. We were hoping you might be able to clear it up for us."

Jubal stood up and said, "I'll try. What's the question, Eilie?"

"How did Uncle Connor know that the Quortrin was dangerous?" she asked. "You told me that only Fledglings with human blood had gifts. Uncle Connor was pure Welkin. But he knew before anyone that there was a reason to be scared of the Quortrin."

"I've been wondering that myself," Jubal answered. "I'm not really sure why or how he had that premonition. Maybe it was the simple fact that Connor was the first Welkin to be born on Earth. Here's what I do know; I have traveled billions of miles and visited over a dozen planets, but none of them is as special as Earth. I think being born here makes you special. Earth people seem to be born with all sorts of gifts. And you don't have to be a Fledgling to have gifts. I have seen some remarkable things in my travels. But I have never seen as many gifted people as the ones on this planet. Maybe someday everyone will discover their own gifts and come to appreciate the gifts they see in others."

"Will you tell me about your travels, Grandpa?" Eilie asked.

"The next time you come for a visit, I will tell you about all of the marvels I have seen just in our small corner of the galaxy," he said.

"I would like to hear those stories, too," Jake said. "I think I'm finally ready to listen."

"I would like that," Jubal said with a smile.

"Daddy, I figured out what letter the third set of wings on my bracelet is," Eilie said, holding up her left wrist. "It's an M."

"What does the M stand for?" Jake asked.

"Mother," she answered. "The wings stand for Eilie Wingfield, Mother."

"I like that," Jake said. "Who would have guessed it was an ID bracelet?"

"I suppose I could remake it for you with the wings turned to show the letters better," Jubal offered.

"I think I like it the way it is," Eilie said. "It's like a secret code only we know."

"You know, I'm not really sure I like you being a mother to two space ships," Jake said.

"Why, Daddy?" she asked.

"Because that makes me a grandfather," Jake replied. "I am way too young to have grandchildren."

"You're over 150 years old," Eilie said with a laugh.

"Yes, but your grandfather is much older," Jake bantered back. "I really don't want to be a grandfather until I'm his age."

"How old are you, Grandpa?" she asked. "I never thought about it, but you've been on Earth for over five hundred years. How old were you when you got here?"

"OK, I think it's time we head back to the house," Jubal said. "I have a lot of paperwork to catch up on."

The doorbell rang at Carol Wingfield's house. She opened the door to find Eilie and Jake standing there. She reached out for Eilie and squeezed her tightly. "I have missed you so much. I was worried sick. I called and called. I even went to your dad's house."

"I'm OK, Mom," Eilie assured her. "I'm really fine."

"Sorry, but my cell phone was dropped into the San Miguel River," Jake said sheepishly.

"You!" Carol yelled at Jake. "I am so mad at you I could spit. What's the idea of not letting me know you left early for Colorado? And why didn't you get Eilie to Dr. Oliphant? She could have a serious kidney infection. Did she even see a doctor in Colorado? I can't believe you have been so irresponsible."

Jake held up his hand, trying to quell the rant. "I apologize for everything, and, yes, I was irresponsible. But we have some things the three of us need to discuss. Can we come in and talk, please?"

Carol stood aside, holding the door and motioned them in. She closed the door and leaned her forehead against the door frame in an effort to calm herself before she turned to face them. She was overly stressed, but she was not going to let Jake off lightly. She turned around to look at them and realized they were both floating three feet off the floor. She could not speak. She felt her knees weaken, and she fell backward against the door. Slowly, with her back on the door, she lowered herself to the floor and stared in absolute disbelief.

Eilie and Jake descended. Eilie went to her mom and sat beside her. Jake followed, and all three were sitting on the floor of the foyer.

"OK. I was going to ask you to sit down," Eilie said, "so this will work. Mom, I can fly. So can Daddy. It's OK. We're not freaks or anything. Daddy and I are aliens. We're not like brain-eating aliens or anything like that. We're just good old American aliens. Well, except Daddy was born in England. But, he's an American now. Anyway, we're back, and everything is OK, and all the bad guys are in jail. And, oh yeah, Uncle Jubal is really my grandpa, and I have these two other uncles who aren't aliens, but they are over 500 years old, and Daddy got to meet his brother for the first time, but he died, and I got to fly a spaceship. Aren't you going to say anything?"

"Honey, I think you covered everything so fast you fried her brain," Jake said. "Carol, we have a lot to talk about. Let's go into the living room. It's time you know how remarkable our daughter truly is. And it's time you know the secret I kept from you and why I had to."

Jake stood up and took Carol's hand. Eilie rose and took her other hand. They pulled her up, guided her to the living room, and positioned her on the sofa. Jake took a chair opposite the sofa, and Eilie sat beside her mom.

"Alright, Carol," Jake began, "I think the best way to do this is for you to ask questions, and we'll answer them point by point."

Carol still felt unsettled but managed to ask, "Eilie can fly?"

Eilie answered, "Yes, I can, Mom. And it is so cool."

"I saw you float, just now," Carol said. "Is that what you mean? You can levitate?"

"When we talk about flying we are really talking about all of it," Jake explained. "Levitating, floating, hovering, soaring, and flying. We have an extra gland which produces a hormone that creates an abatement field around our cells and in our blood. The field is like a torsion wave that temporarily abates gravity."

"I will pretend I understood that," Carol said. "How fast can you fly?"

"Not like in the movies, but about as fast as a person can run," Jake said. "If we go up really high and shut down the field we can free-fall like a skydiver. You can get some pretty good speed then. But that's just falling, not really flying."

"I want to try that," Eilie said with excitement. "Will you show me that trick please?"

"One thing at a time, Little," Jake cautioned. "Let's stay focused on answering your mom's questions."

Eilie nodded in agreement.

"You have this gland because you are an alien," Carol said. "You're not human?"

"Genetically, I'm half-human," Jake replied.

"Did it not occur to you to mention that while we were dating?" Carol asked.

"I have lived as a human since 1862," Jake answered. "The only time I think about being alien is when I fly."

"1862?" she asked. "I thought we were the same age, so obviously, you age very slowly. What other things can you do? What other powers do you have?"

"I can answer that one," Eilie said excitedly. "Grandpa explained it to me. We don't have the power of flight; we have the ability to fly. It's a naturally occurring ability. Just like if someone can lift up the end of a car that has fallen on a friend, an adrenaline surge can give a person superhuman strength. Our ascendal glands give us a natural ability. So, we don't have any powers at all."

For the next two hours, Jake and Eilie carefully answered all of Carol's questions, and gradually, Carol became more relaxed. She was not happy about having a daughter who could fly, but she knew she would accept whatever Eilie was or chose to be because that's what one does when one is a mom.

After many questions and lots of patient answers, Carol was finally smiling again, and Eilie told her about meeting girls her age at the Gathering and how they would be email pals. She talked about baby animals at the ranch and how she had the best time ever. Carol did frown, however, when Eilie mentioned letting Uncle Joe teach her to fly airplanes. For all the other outlandish things she had heard today that one was just not acceptable, at least not this year.

Carol got up to get some refreshments and paused in the kitchen. She seemed to be having difficulty expressing a thought. "You know, I'm not sure how I am going to explain all this to Paul."

Eilie and Jake both stood up and moved toward the kitchen. "Carol, you cannot tell anyone about any of this," Jake said very slowly.

"Oh, I understand not telling the neighbors," Carol said. "They can't keep a secret. But you can't expect me to keep all this from the man I am about to marry."

Jake looked sternly at Carol and firmly said, "Yes, I can. And I do. That is exactly what I expect you to do. You cannot share any of this with anyone."

"Mom, Daddy is right," Eilie added. "You would not just put me in danger; you could put everyone in danger."

"Eilie, I would never put you in danger," Carol said. "But we're talking about Paul. He's going to be your stepfather. You have to trust him."

"Not with this," Eilie quickly responded. "Trusting him is not the issue. The issue is trusting everyone he knows. Everyone he tells secrets to."

"Carol," Jake said, "for over five hundred years, my family has guarded this secret. Not just to protect ourselves, but to protect the world. Things have changed in the last five centuries, and new technologies put us at an even greater risk. I learned the hard way that something as simple as a text message to a relative could be turned against us. One of our own tried to hurt us. Can you imagine what total strangers would do? We could be turned into an enemy overnight simply because we're different. We could be herded into camps for our 'protection.' We could be marched into hospitals to be studied for the 'common good.' I saw this kind of thinking as it was happening seventy-five years ago."

"Don't you think you're overreacting?" she asked.

"No, I don't," he answered. "I know what can happen with a slip of the tongue. People fear what they don't understand. And, historically speaking, we are not that far removed from public hangings and lynching. They were still being carried out last century. So let me make this point very clear; unless you want your daughter to be the object of a mob's pursuit or a scientific study, you have to promise that you never share anything with anyone."

Eilie's eyes were red and near tears as she listened to her father's ominous warnings. Carol was close to tearing as well. She walked over to her daughter and hugged her. "I love Paul. I don't want to keep any secrets from him."

Eilie looked up at Carol and said, "Mom, sometimes keeping a secret is the most loving thing you can do."

Carol stroked Eilie's face and wiped a tear from her cheek. She turned to Jake and said, "I divorced you because you kept secrets from me. Now you finally share these secrets and ask me to keep them from a new husband."

"That's called irony," Eilie said softly.

Carol chuckled. "Yes, I suppose it is," she said. "Alright, I promise you both, I will never share any of this with anyone at any time. But I want a promise in return. I want both of you to promise me that I will never be left out of the loop again." She looked directly at Jake. "Anything that relates to our daughter's welfare; any freaky little alien whatever that affects her, I want to know when it happens, not after."

"You have my word," Jake said.

Then she turned to Eilie. "I do not want you to take any of this lightly. If your safety is at stake, then I want you to protect yourself at all costs. The Wingfields may have hundreds of years of practice at safeguarding themselves, but you don't. Do what they tell you. Obviously, they know what they're doing."

"You have my word," Eilie intoned.

"And one more thing," Carol said. "None of this is easy for me. It may take a while to adjust to everything. Promise me you'll be patient and that you won't expect me to understand it all at once. Please."

Together, Eilie and Jake said, "We promise."

Gracie was standing at the bay window as Jubal walked into the study. She had a solemn expression that conveyed neither worry nor happiness, but he understood the look. He had seen the same expression on his late wife Grace's face when he and Jake were butting heads a hundred-forty years earlier.

"Well?" he asked.

"I have finished the analysis, Jubal," Gracie said.

"What does it show?" he sighed.

"Your concern seems to be correct," she replied. "From every test I have run, the results are the same."

"I was afraid of that," he said. "No Welkin has ever merged with a ship. When Eilie told me she merged with the Quortrin, I knew there had to be a side effect."

"There was, Jubal," Gracie said, moving closer to him. "The comparison to cellular activity in the ships is identical. It's as if she was a part of them. She has retained enough of her human DNA to be still considered human. But her Welkin DNA has mutated beyond anything imaginable. It appears the ships' legend of The Mother has become a reality. For all practical purposes, she is their mother, and they will respond to her accordingly. But there is one more change you didn't anticipate."

"What else?" he asked with apprehension.

"Do you remember when Eilie was six years old, she had her appendix removed?" Gracie asked.

Jubal nodded his head. "Yes, her body saved her from the infection by encapsulating the toxins."

"Apparently, she began mutating sooner than we thought," she said. "When she was in Connor's house, and the bracelet injected the nanobots into her, I was not able to maintain contact very long because her antibodies were so effective at destroying the bots." Gracie did her best to place her holographic hand on Jubal's shoulder. "Eilie is now immortal."

Eilie was at her dad's house for another week. He told her they would hang around for a few days and unwind from all the excitement of Colorado. He also said they could take Francie with them to the zoo on Saturday. Eilie was glad to be back in her room and her bed. Traveling was fun, but coming home was the best part.

She had unpacked her bags and put her mementos in special places around the room. The marshal's badge Hoyt Kendrick had given her was pinned to the pink cowgirl hat she got from Uncle Joe. Her favorite item was the bracelet from Grandpa that was still on her left wrist. It saved her and her dad. She ran her fingers over the three sets of wings and smiled at the memory of how she had decided they were also letters. It gave her comfort to know that Gracie would be close when she needed her. Then, a pleasant thought crossed Eilie's mind. She quickly brushed her teeth and changed into her pajamas. She turned off the room lights, pulled back the covers, took the laptop off her desk, and jumped into bed.

She made sure she was connected to the internet and typed in GRACIE I NEED YOU. The computer made some bizarre noises, and it looked like several different programs were trying to open all at once. Then, on the screen, Eilie saw Gracie.

"Are you alright?" Gracie asked. "Do I need to send help?"

"I'm OK," Eilie said. "I just missed you."

"You have only been gone from the ranch for eight hours and thirteen minutes," Gracie said. "It seems unlikely you would miss anyone so soon."

"I just wanted to talk," Eilie said. "You're not busy, are you?"

"I am never too busy to talk with you," Gracie replied with a wink.

"I wanted to thank you again for all your help," Eilie said.

"It was my pleasure to serve you, Eilie," Gracie said. "Are you preparing to go back to school?"

"Not yet," Eilie answered. "School only ended two weeks ago. We still have a few more weeks of summer vacation."

"What are your plans for the remaining time, then?" Gracie asked.

"We'll do the usual stuff, like going to the zoo and the aquarium," Eilie responded. "On the 4th of July, we'll watch the fireworks show on the river. We'll also see some baseball games downtown. I know Daddy will want us to spend a weekend in Eureka Springs. It's a short drive from here. I know Francie and I will do a lot of stuff together like swimming and sleepovers. And the big thing will be in August when my mom has her wedding. By the time she and Paul get back from their honeymoon, school will start again, and I will be in fifth grade."

"Well," Gracie said, "it certainly sounds like you have many plans to round out your summer."

"I guess so," Eilie said with a little hesitation.

"Why do you sound unsure?" Gracie asked.

"The trip to Tutela just makes everything else seem so dull," Eilie confessed. "It's hard to get excited about the zoo when I know I can fly. And I flew a spaceship. Being home just seems boring now."

"I suppose it does," Gracie said. "But if you had ice cream three times a day, it would no longer be a treat. It would just be boring."

"Ice cream can't be boring," Eilie said.

"How often do you have ice cream?" Gracie inquired.

"At least once a week, I guess," Eilie responded.

"So you still think of it as a treat," Gracie said. "If you only had it once a month, it would be a special treat. Suppose you could only taste ice cream once a year. How special would it be then?"

"It would be a super special treat then," Eilie answered.

"It is very easy to think of the things, events, and people in your life as not being special because you see them often," Gracie explained. "You take your parents for granted because they are always there. You take your friends and classmates for granted because they are always there. You only get to come to the ranch once a year, so you think of that as a special trip. But if you lived here then going to Tulsa once a year would be a special trip. Do you understand that what you do every day is special, too? No matter how boring or common something seems, it is special. The simple fact that you are experiencing it makes it special."

"Everything can't be special, Gracie," Eilie argued.

"Do you think about your ability to walk as being special?" Gracie asked.

Eilie shook her head.

"To someone confined to a wheelchair, it is," Gracie said. "They would love to have your special ability to walk. There are people who envy your special ability to hear and to see because they cannot. If people learned you could fly, they would want your ability. To them, it would be special. Every skill, every ability, every talent, and every gift that people possess is more special to others than to themselves. If you simply shift the limited way you see your life and your world, you will come to realize that every little thing is special, because you experience it."

"I never thought of it that way before," Eilie said. "I don't want to take my family or my friends for granted. I understand what you're saying, but I'm not sure I can remember to make everything special. I will probably forget. Will you remind me if I forget?"

"I promise I will," Gracie said. "Will you make a promise to me?"

"About what?" Eilie asked.

"Promise me that you will live each day with the same sense of wonder and excitement you felt the first time you flew," Gracie said.

Eilie felt warmth embrace her. She remembered that feeling. She knew exactly what Gracie was asking her to do. And amazingly, she knew she could keep such a promise. She really wanted never to lose that incredible feeling she experienced when she first hung in the air. She made an X over her heart and said, "I promise. Can I ask a favor, Gracie?"

"Of course," she answered.

"Grandpa used my grandmother's picture for you," Eilie said. "So you look like she did when she lived a long time ago. Daddy said she had a beautiful voice and she would sing to him when he was little. Could you find some songs from my grandmother's time and sing them for me?"

Gracie smiled and said, "I have located several ballads and lullabies from England in the last half of the nineteenth century. Would you like me to list them for you?"

"Just pick some and sing them, please," Eilie said. "And, if it's no trouble, could you keep singing until I fall asleep?

"It will be my pleasure to sing you to sleep," Gracie said.

Eilie moved deeper under her bed covers and found a snug spot for her head on the pillow. She turned toward Gracie's image and pulled the laptop closer. She heard the first notes of an old song and then she heard the most angelic voice she could imagine as Gracie sang for her. The melody was soothing, and Gracie's voice seemed hypnotic. Before the last chords of the song were finished, Eilie had drifted off to the deepest sleep she had ever known.

Epilogue

Eilie and Francie were adjusting their costumes and hair. Francie was wearing a tuxedo with a bow tie and a top hat, and she was carrying a magician's wand. Eilie was in a long, flowing white gown that she had worn last spring at her ballet recital. Her hair was pulled back, and she had a wreath of white flowers circling her face. Backstage, at the first talent show of the new school year, all the other performers were quietly chatting and waiting for their curtain call, which would happen right after Eilie and Francie performed their act.

Jake was adjusting the cables and making sure the halter wires were hidden completely by Eilie's costume. Out in the audience, on the front row, Frank and Katherine Forbes were sitting next to the newlyweds, Paul and Carol Simmons. Mrs. Clarkson approached the microphone and said, "We have had many talented performers over the years, but I know we have never had an act like this one. I think you all are about to be amazed. Please welcome Francie Forbes and Eilie Wingfield as they perform something magical."

Mrs. Clarkson took the microphone stand offstage, and the curtains opened, showing Eilie and Francie standing center stage. Music began to play, and Francie stepped forward and bowed. She pointed her wand at Eilie, who walked forward and stood beside her. Francie faced Eilie and made circular motions with her wand around Eilie's head. Eilie seemed to go into a trance and closed her eyes.

The music grew louder, and Francie made upward motions with both her hands. Slowly, Eilie rose into the air and seemed to hang about three feet off the stage. The crowd gave an audible gasp, and then applauded. The music was building to a crescendo as Francie made broad sweeping motions with her arms, and Eilie began to spin, slowly, at first, but then she picked up speed and stopped abruptly. Francie waved her wand and Eilie's head lowered to the same level as her feet, so she was floating horizontally to the floor about three feet up. Francie picked up a plastic hoop from the floor and passed it all around Eilie to suggest that there were no wires. The audience applauded again.

Paul leaned over to Carol and said, "Jake is doing an incredible job. I can't see any wires."

"He's very good at hiding things," she replied.

Francie tossed the hoop to the back of the stage and again made broad sweeping motions with her arms. Eilie's arms extended outward like airplane wings and she flipped over, facing the floor. Then, in a broad sweeping arc, she flew out over the audience and returned to Francie, where she landed feet first on the stage. Francie woke Eilie from her trance, and they both took a bow as the audience rose to their feet in thunderous applause.

Backstage, Jake was rolling up the harness cables, when a boy, who appeared to be Eilie's age, came up to him and tugged on his shirt. Jake looked down and said, "Yes."

"I know it's done with wires," the boy said.

"Of course it is," Jake confirmed. "You don't believe people can really fly, do you?"

The boy looked closely at the loose wires hanging from the rafters. "When did you unhook her?" he asked.

Jake smiled at the boy and said, "It's all done automatically. We have to be ready for the curtain call."

All the performers joined Eilie and Francie onstage, and they took a group bow. Francie leaned toward Eilie and said, "I can't believe how real your dad made it look. Even right under you, I couldn't see the wires."

"It's like my Uncle Connor said," Eilie replied. "If you're going to do an illusion, make it real."

END

PART ONE